HANNAH MESSENGER

AND THE GODS OF HOCKWOLD

HAVE YOU EVER WONDERED HOW BOOKS ARE MADE?

UCLan Publishing is an award-winning independent publisher specialising in Children's and Young Adult books. Based at The University of Central Lancashire, this Preston-based publisher teaches MA Publishing students how to become industry professionals using the content and resources from its business; students are included at every stage of the publishing process and credited for the work that they contribute.

The business doesn't just help publishing students though. UCLan Publishing has supported the employability and real-life work skills for the University's Illustration, Acting, Translation, Animation, Photography, Film & TV students and many more. This is the beauty of books and stories; they fuel many other creative industries! The MA Publishing students are able to get involved from day one with the business and they acquire a behind the scenes experience of what it is like to work for such a reputable independent.

The MA course was awarded a Times Higher Award (2018) for Innovation in the Arts and the business, UCLan Publishing, was awarded Best Newcomer at the Independent Publishing Guild (2019) for the ethos of teaching publishing using a commercial publishing house. As the business continues to grow, so too does the student experience upon entering this dynamic Masters course.

www.uclanpublishing.com
www.uclanpublishing.com/courses/
uclanpublishing@uclan.ac.uk

For the kind kids, who know that a friend
is the best thing you can be

Hannah Messenger is a uclanpublishing book

First published in Great Britain in 2024 by
uclanpublishing
University of Central Lancashire
Preston, PR1 2HE, UK

Set in 10/16pt Kingfisher by Becky Chilcott.

A CIP catalogue record for this book is available from the British Library.

Printed and bound in Great Britain by Clays Ltd, Elcograf S.p.A.

BRYONY PEARCE

HANNAH MESSENGER

AND THE GODS OF HOCKWOLD

ILLUSTRATED BY CLAIRE POWELL

uclanpublishing

INTRODUCTION

BY HANNAH MESSENGER, AGED 11

I'M GUESSING that most of you know that Zeus is King of the Gods. But what you probably don't know is that he's retired. That's right. When humans invented the nuclear bomb, he started yelling rude things about atoms and hung up his thunderbolt.

When Zeus retired as King of the Gods, he relocated to a taverna in Greece where he drank a lot of ouzo, ate a lot of baklava and chased a lot of waitresses around tables.

The eating and drinking were fine (except for his expanding waistline), but his wife, Hera, was deeply unhappy about the waitresses (see *Great Kefalonia Earthquake*, 1953).

She gave him an ultimatum: relocate to a place of *her* choosing, or face retirement alone.

And that is how Zeus, King of the Gods, and Hera, Goddess of Marriage and Family, ended up retiring to a small village in Cambridgeshire called Hockwold-cum-Wilton, which has a notable lack of ouzo and baklava, and absolutely no waitresses under the age of fifty.

Over time, a number of other gods joined them. Even some who I would call 'god-adjacent' turned up, like the descendants of Prometheus. (Prometheus stole fire from the gods, gave it to humans, and in return got nailed to a cliff for thousands of years. I never said the gods were *nice*.)

It became quite a community.

And this is where I come in. My name is Hannah Messenger. I'm eleven years old and I'm the great-granddaughter of Zeus and Hera, and granddaughter of Hermes, the messenger god, who gave up on humanity when emails were invented. He doesn't live in Hockwold, due to the fact that, well, he's kind of a trickster, and one of his most recent tricks got him put in time-out. OK, prison. It's a bit embarrassing. We don't talk about it.

The last thing to mention is that when I was little, Hera took what you might call the ultimate retirement. And because Hermes' magic staff can open any door, including the one between life and death, and because the staff is currently hanging in our lounge, Zeus asked Dad to try and bring her back from the dead. So, Hera's in an urn in our spare room right now and Dad has been working on resurrection spells for as long as I can remember.

Funnily enough, Zeus hasn't even *tried* to chase a waitress since.

So that's how most of the Greek gods, and their hangers-on, and their families, ended up in a tiny village near Cambridge. We don't get involved in the problems of humans. There's no point. Any solution we could come up with, they've either already gone one bigger (see *nuclear bombs*), or already destroyed (see *rainforests*). The local council is an absolute battleground though.

And so my story starts, on the day I come into my powers.

CHAPTER ONE

THE DAY I come into my powers, nobody notices, because my great-grandmother explodes and almost takes the roof off the house. Again.

As I hover there, a couple of centimetres above the ground, Mum rushes into the second bedroom with the fire extinguisher.

Dad is sitting in a ring of scorched carpet, without his eyebrows, glaring at the urn on top of the mantlepiece.

"She's doing this on purpose!" he yells, pointing at the urn. As I watch, a handful of ashes whirl into it and the lid slams closed with a snap. The bowl on the table, which must have recently contained the ashes, is in pieces.

"Of course she is, dear." Mum sprays foam around the room, starting with the glowing shards of ceramic and ending with Dad's smouldering jumper. "She said she wanted a little rest."

"A little rest? It's been *eight years*! She has to come back. I can't tell Zeus I've failed *again*. And we need her on the council. Some of the descendants are saying we should get involved in human politics, and she was the only one able to rein any of them in." Dad jumps to his feet and notices me by the door. "Isn't it a school day?"

"Yes, but . . ." I gesture helplessly at my feet, but at that moment the little flare of power that had been lifting me up fizzles out and I drop to the floor with a thump.

"Don't jump on the landing," Mum says, without even turning around. She's stalking a glowing ember that has escaped her hose. "You'll wake your brother. Honestly, Hannah, you get more like your grandad every day. Thinking only about yourself!"

I don't say that if Henry hasn't been woken by Dad's explosion, he is unlikely to be woken by the soft thud of my slippers.

"Go on," Dad says. "Get dressed quickly, and I'll make your favourite."

"You don't *make* Coco Pops." I roll my eyes, still stinging from Mum's remark. "You just add milk."

"That's gourmet cooking as far as your father's concerned," Mum says, turning to face me. "You're still in your PJs, Hannah. You're going to be late!"

I sigh. She's right, I'm going to be late.

"And get that *tortoise* out of here!" Dad snaps, pointing at Dolio. He's sitting on the hearth gazing at me mournfully. "Honestly!" Dad breathes. "That creature. It's always around! I swear it's watching me."

"And they didn't even notice?" My best friend and partner in crime, aka 'that awful boy', aka Dylan Susan (don't ask) Vine, walks beside me towards the bus stop.

"You know what it's like in my house." I sigh. "Dad was trying to bring Hera back to her body again."

"She won't be back until she wants to be back," Dylan says sagely, offering me a strawberry lace. I shake my head and he shrugs, wraps it around his finger and sucks it into his mouth. "So, have you got . . . y'know?"

I pull down my left sock to reveal a five-centimetre cluster of feathers protruding from my ankle bone. Dylan crouches. "Cute."

"They're not even white." I squint at the dirty grey bundle. "I look like a pigeon."

Dylan strokes the downy fluff with one finger, and I giggle. "That tickles." I yank my sock back up.

"Will they get bigger?"

"I'm not sure. Dad's are the size of his hand, so . . . I guess?"

Dylan stands back up. "You're so lucky."

"Yeah, right! I'm meant to be a *messenger*. Even if I could fly faster than an F16 Jet, which I definitely can't with these things," I raise a foot, "I'd still be slower than a text message. I'm *useless*." I gesture at Dylan. "*Your* powers are getting stronger though." A bunch of strawberry laces protrudes from his shirt pocket.

He sniffs. "I make strawberry laces. It's a useless power."

"Not true," I say, poking him. "Everyone loves strawberry laces. *And* you can speak to the dead."

"Have you any idea how *boring* dead people are?" Dylan snaps.

HANNAH MESSENGER

"Tell Laura I love her. Watch out for magpies. Let Martha know I'm watching her and if she doesn't give the silver bracelet to Margery . . ." He stops and blinks. "Is that Dolio?"

Dolio's wrinkled head is poking out of the top of my bag like he's a tiny Extra Terrestrial.

"Dad told me to take him." I give him a little pat and he tries to nip my finger.

"He's *vicious*," Dylan says, backing away from my bag. "I don't know why you like him so much."

I shrug. "Sometimes I think he's the only one in my house who actually listens to me."

"Awright, losers?"

I turn to see Zack and Zane strolling towards us. Zack is a year older than we are, and a golden boy if ever there was one. He is godlike in his good looks: well-built, charming, with white teeth that catch the light. Zane is basically his slightly smaller clone. It's ridiculous.

I nudge Dylan, who is standing awkwardly, staring, one hand caught in the act of trying to smooth his frizzy red hair. "He's nothing more than a toothpaste advert come to life," I whisper, catching his wrist and pulling it to his side. "Boring, predictable and he couldn't love himself more if he was made of chocolate."

Dylan doesn't answer. Instead, he glances at his own too-short trousers and trainers with holes in.

"Check this out, losers!" Zack says, and points a finger at Dylan's feet.

Miniature storm clouds boil above us and a bolt of lightning no bigger than my middle finger hits the ground, charring Dylan's shoes. I smell burning rubber and Dylan leaps on to the grass, stamping madly.

Zane laughs. "Nice one!" Then he looks at me. "Zack's powers turned up at the weekend. There was a huge family party. Huge!"

Dylan bristles. "Yeah? Well, Hannah's got—"

I stamp on his foot. "Congratulations, Zack, that's great."

Zack smirks and points at Dylan again.

I put my hands on my hips. "Stop it!"

"Stop what?" Zack looks innocent. "Anyway, what are you going to do about it – take a *message* to your mummy?"

Zane laughs. Neither of them are funny.

"Give us some then," Zane says to Dylan, and holds out a hand.

Dylan sighs and pulls a tangle of laces from his pocket. He hands them over and immediately his pocket is full again.

"Worst gift *ever!*" Zane says, stuffing five into his mouth at once.

"Yeah? Well, you seem to be enjoying it," I growl.

Zack points at me, and it goes grey overhead. I close my mouth. "Thought so," he says smugly. The two shoulder-barge their way past Dylan, and I catch his elbow as he stumbles. As Zack and Zane reach the end of the road, they start high fiving one another and the clouds that had gathered above our heads dissolve like bath bombs.

"I don't want to go to school today," Dylan says suddenly.

I look at him. There are tears in his eyes.

"Dylan—"

"No, listen! You need to practise your new power, right? What are we going to learn at school that's more important than that? Yet another lesson about the Titans? Another drama class where Zack gets to kill us with a wooden sword then gross-kiss Amy Fairchild?" He grimaces.

"Well..."

"He melted my trainers, Hannah! Come on, let's go to the Fens. We won't bump into anyone out there. All the grown-ups are going to be at another council meeting. You seriously want to just ... go to school? On the day you got your powers?"

I hesitate. He's got a point. Usually on a gift day (the day you get your powers) the whole family celebrates – a day off school, a restaurant dinner, the whole nine-yards. Mine gave me a bowl of Coco Pops and a headache.

"OK," I say. "Let's do it."

CHAPTER TWO

WE HIDE behind a bush until we are certain that everyone heading for school has gone past. Then we sprint in the opposite direction. I giggle and Dylan grabs my hand, pulling me along.

Power puffs at my feet like a gust of wind and I find myself half-running, half-gliding in that weird way you do when you're dreaming. I imagine myself walking on the moon, taking huge, bouncing steps, and soon I outpace Dylan and drop his hand.

Before I know it, I'm past the village green and the huge metal gate that leads to the mansion housing the retired gods (avoided by anyone with a sense of self-preservation) and have reached the marker stone. I sit on it and wait, watching Dylan run panting up to me as I stroke Dolio's protruding beak.

The marker stone is a large square block with a faded carving of ram's horns in the centre. Humans think it marks the boundary between the old villages of Hockwold and Wilton. It does. But it also protects Hockwold from prying human eyes.

Residents of Hockwold (like me and Dylan) can stroll in and out of the village, but ordinary humans trying to enter get distracted. Many a confused tourist has found themselves inexplicably fascinated by the fifteenth-century pews in St James's church, Wilton, when they had intended to explore Hockwold Hall.

More importantly, no one outside the barrier can see anything 'godlike' going on. From the other side of the marker our village appears to be normal, and Zeus and the rest can safely blow stuff up (this happens surprisingly often) without humans calling the emergency services.

Also, it's a nice place to sit.

Dylan reaches the stone and turns around. "Hey," he says. "Your dad must have been ploughing some serious power into his spell this morning. Your roof is totally on fire."

"It's not *on fire*," I say, checking on our cottage. It's one of the more normal looking houses in Hockwold: we have the bare minimum in the way of Greek columns, and Mum replaced the statue of Hermes with one of a constipated lion after 'the incident'. "It's smouldering, at best," I say.

Dylan starts moonwalking backwards past the stone. "I love this bit," he says, pointing. "Hockwold, retirement home of the gods." He takes the final step so that he's on the other side of the stone. "Hockwold, boring human village. It's genius!"

I nod. I wish I was like Hockwold: something powerful disguised as something ordinary. But, if anything, I suspect I'm the other

11

way around: something ordinary made to look interesting with a little bit of useless power.

The thought makes me pat Dolio again.

"Come *on*, Hannah," Dylan says.

There's a stone sword in the middle of the village green, marking the place Hera was standing when she declared Hockwold her new home. I fix my eyes on it, then, like Dylan, I walk backwards. You don't *have* to walk backwards when leaving Hockwold, but it helps with the nausea if you pick a point and keep an eye on it when you cross the boundary.

There's a tingle across my shoulders that feels as if I've touched an electric fence, and then I'm seeing Hockwold as the humans do.

The sword becomes a cross. It's a small change among lots of big ones: Zane's house, Hockwold Hall, has transformed from a palatial monstrosity with more columns than the Acropolis, into an Elizabethan mansion with white-edged windows and a crenellated tower. The wrestling arena has become a cricket pitch, and the temple a rather pretty church with carved angels on the roof and a sign saying, 'Saint Peter's'. Only the gateway to reach the home of Zeus remains unchanged: a tall metal 'keep out' with a design you shouldn't look at too closely, if you don't want nightmares.

I feel a bit like I've been on a roller coaster after a dozen doughnuts. Dylan rubs my back until I feel less green, then we turn to the road that leads towards the countryside, otherwise known as the Fens.

I clear my throat. "You shouldn't listen to Zack and Zane,

you know." I give Dylan's hand a squeeze. "Just because Zack can shoot lightning bolts! He says *your* power is useless, but what use is *his,* really? I mean, OK, if he ever goes camping and wants to make s'mores, it'll be useful, but otherwise . . ."

Dylan sniffs.

"Seriously, Dylan. Is anyone we know *really* that powerful, when you consider the stuff humans can do now? I mean look at the internet, space shuttles, antibiotics—"

Dylan sighs. "Try telling Zack! No one will ever respect me so long as all I can do is make sweets from thin air and talk to dead grandmas."

"I love your sweets," I say, but all he does is nod.

We reach the outskirts of the village without anyone yelling something like, "Why aren't you kids in school?" and I relax.

"We're going to the Tree, right?" I say.

Dylan looks at me like I've lost my mind. "Where else would we go?"

The Tree has been a not-so-secret meeting ground for Hockwold kids wanting to bunk off school since *forever.*

We find the footpath that will take us to the field, where the Tree stands as a lonely sentinel against the horizon, and amble there between the reeds and sedges.

The Fens, if you can imagine it, are ninety per cent sky. They are so flat that clouds form most of the landscape, either looming above or reflected in pools. I think that's why Hera chose this area: squint and it's like being in heaven.

A tourist on a bike appears from around a corner, zips past

and vanishes, then we're alone. Stiff grasses brush our ankles, and birds call overhead. There is a patch of rushes to our right and dragonflies flit from one side to the other.

As we reach the boards that an enterprising teen placed over a particularly boggy section of the footpath, a butterfly lands on my bag.

Dolio moves surprisingly quickly. Then he looks at me innocently, with orange wings protruding from either side of his beak.

"That's gross!" Dylan says.

The butterfly vanishes.

Dylan narrows his eyes. "I thought tortoises were vegetarian."

"Dolio eats insects too. Don't you, Dolio? I just wish he'd leave the pretty ones alone."

Dolio gives the tortoise equivalent of a shrug. If he had lips, I just know he'd be licking them. I shake my head, then look up.

"We're here."

In front of us the Tree wraps its branches around the clouds. I swallow.

"I'm not sure I want to practise flying, after all," I say.

"Rubbish." Dylan drags me forwards. "What's the worst that can happen?"

CHAPTER THREE

"**THINK LIKE** Iron Man," Dylan shouts, as I wobble five centimetres above the ground. "Pretend you've got thrusters on your hands. Balance! Balance!"

"Balance? Ha!" I mutter. My stomach lurches, my power gives a sort of hiccup and I rocket upwards. My head races towards a branch, I twist to avoid it, yelp and swing forward. For a moment, I feel like one of the players on Dylan's old football table. Then I'm dangling in midair from my ankles.

My head is about level with Dylan's. He's grinning.

"Stop laughing!" The blood is rushing to my head and the tiny wings on my ankles are flapping like mad.

"Can't you come down?" he asks.

I think *Down*, but nothing happens. "I'm getting dizzy! Help!"

"Picture heavy things?"

"Stones, rocks, mountains!" I bob higher. "*Dylan!*"

He jumps and catches my fingers. Then he stiffens and lets me go.

"What are you doing? Hold on!"

Something catches in my hair and flaps madly in my face. "*Argh!*" I try to shove the thing away. It's all feathers, beak and claws. I can't see it, but it's nipping at my fingers and cooing like mad.

"What in the name of *Hera*? Dylan!"

A pair of red eyes bore into mine, claws rake my nose . . . and then the bird is gone.

Blood drips into my eye, and I manage to raise my head and watch as the little turd finds a tree branch and sits there, puffing out its chest and fluffing its wings. I had never realised doves could look so evil.

I look back down again, really dizzy now. If I'm going to be sharing the skies with demons like that, then I'm *definitely* over flying. I spot Dylan staring at someone just beyond the trunk of the tree.

"What are *you* doing here?" he demands, his tone oddly high-pitched.

"I could ask you the same thing!" comes a familiar voice.

"Oh *no!*" I fling my feet around until I'm able to turn. And there she is, Amy Fairchild, in all her smug, perfect-looking glory, standing on the other side of the Tree.

"We were here first!" Dylan says. Is he . . . *blushing*?

"Well, I *planned* to be here first," she snaps. I notice Amy has beads in her hair – like she needs to be prettier! Then her eyes meet mine and she bursts out laughing. "What are you *doing*, Hannah?" she sneers. "That's pathetic."

The worst thing is, she's right. I'm dangling a couple of metres above the ground by my tiny ankle wings, with blood dripping off the end of my nose and into my hair. It *is* pathetic.

"Shut up," I mutter.

"I mean, *seriously*!" She giggles. "I thought *I* was having a bad day."

I glower at Dylan. "Are you going to help me down or not? Because if you don't, I warn you, I'm going to throw up."

Dylan's eyes widen. He hops and catches my hand again. My tiny wings work harder, as if to fight him, and Amy sighs loudly. Then she's adding her weight to Dylan's and I'm hitting the floor. The air rushes out of me and I grab a clump of sedge, gripping it to prevent my power from launching me skywards again.

I cling to the ground, panting, then look up. Dylan isn't paying me any attention; he's staring at Amy with his mouth open.

I blink, and then I see what he's seeing. The bird from the Tree, and two other plump doves, are fluttering in happy loops around Amy's head, and she's shuffling her feet, as if she daren't stop moving. Wherever Amy's feet touch the earth, little shoots are showing.

"What are those?" I point, and Amy groans and jumps to another spot. Behind her, the shoots start to grow into plants, sprouting first leaves, then thorns. I dive to scoop my bag up, checking that Dolio is still inside and slotting my arms into the straps. "What's going on?"

Amy sighs, as one of the bushes starts to flower.

Dylan laughs. "You're growing roses!"

"I know!" Amy snaps. Then she hops on to an oak root. She checks her feet and sighs with relief. "It only seems to happen if I touch the actual ground."

Dylan shuffles his feet. "Congratulations, I guess. I didn't know you'd developed your powers."

Amy glowers. "*Great* powers! If I'm not dodging rose bushes, I'm cleaning bird poop out of my hair." She waves, trying to scare the birds that are happily circling her head. They avoid her hands and land on a branch, billing and cooing at her with stupid adoration. Then, as if to prove her point, one of them relieves itself on her right shoulder. Her shoulders sag. "What am I going to do? I can't live like this!"

"It doesn't happen to your mum, does it?" Dylan frowns. "I mean, I'd have noticed. Wouldn't you have noticed, Hannah?"

I nod. "Definitely."

"She says it'll just be until I can learn to control it," Amy mutters. "She's delighted, of course. We had pizza."

"Of course you did." I glance at Dylan, and he grimaces. I look back at Amy. "So, you're here to try and work out how to control your power?"

She nods. "Seemed like a good idea. And now that I *am* here, you can go and find somewhere else to do your . . . thing. All right?" She folds her arms.

"Hang on a minute!" I fold my own arms right back at her. "We were here first. And we need the Tree just as much as you do."

"There are lots of trees." Amy gestures at the wide, open field. The field with no other trees in it. "Find another one."

"You're so selfish," I shout. "I can't believe I was feeling sorry for you!"

"*You* feeling sorry for *me*?" Amy glares, and above her head, six red eyes fix on me with identical expressions of outrage. "As if I need sympathy from *you*, Hannah Messenger! Your grandad's a *thief*!"

I gasp as she points at me. Then she turns to Dylan.

"And do you even know where your grandad is? Last seen partying in Mexico, wasn't he?" She sneers. "At least Aphrodite is modelling in Europe, doing something *cool*. You're losers, from whole lines of losers. I don't need your sympathy, I don't need your help and I don't need *you*!"

The doves hurl themselves from the branch above her in a flurry of feathers and frantic poop. She yelps, but they aren't coming for her, they're coming for me; wings pumping, claws extended, their eyes red pinpoints of malice.

I scream, torn between anger at her words and terror of her birds, and throw my hands over my face. Then, my power *burps*. The next thing I know I'm flying towards the top of the Tree, wobbling like crazy as I try to keep my balance. Wind rushes through my hair and I shriek as Amy's homicidal aviary comes at me again. I twist and am, once more, upside down. Only this time I'm wearing my bag.

"Dolio!"

He drops like a stone from the open flap, legs pumping.

"Dylan, catch him!"

Dylan dives across a rosebush and thuds between two roots with his arms outstretched. Dolio plops into his palms.

"Is he all right, Dylan? Is Dolio OK?"

"I think so." Dylan exhales shakily as he gets to his feet. Then he puts Dolio carefully between the roots and turns to Amy. "What was that? You almost killed Dolio!"

That reminds me how angry I am with her. Amy's mean, she used her power to set her birds on me and she almost killed Dolio!

The angrier I get, the higher I rise. Desperately, I make a grab for a cluster of twigs and find my hands filled with leaves. "*Help!*"

The leaves tear from the twigs, my feet burst through the canopy and now there is nothing between my feet and the open sky. Amy's stupid doves perch on top of the tree, satisfied now that they've driven me away from the object of their affection.

I don't know how far my little pigeon wings will take me – but I do know that if I keep rising, at some point I'll either freeze or run out of oxygen. I can't remember which comes first but, if I'm honest, neither seems like a great way to go.

Just as I'm thinking this, my power burps and I rise a little further.

CHAPTER FOUR

"HANNAH!" DYLAN throws himself at the oak and starts to climb. He isn't going to be fast enough to reach me. I'm still heading upwards, like a balloon without a string. I windmill my arms and legs frantically, but nothing makes a difference.

Amy is gawping at me, getting smaller by the moment. "Hannah," she shouts. "You have to *calm down!*"

Tears spill over my forehead and into my hair. Is she *kidding*?

"Unless you want to try and catch a passing plane, listen to me." She waves her arms for emphasis. "Mum told me controlling my powers was about controlling my emotions. Being calm. Maybe it's the same for you. So – *calm down!*"

Calm down? I am *so* much higher than the tree now.

I see Dylan, as a flash of red hair below. He's reached the highest point he can climb – any higher and the branches won't hold his weight. He's reaching for me, as if he can will his arms to grow longer.

"You just have to get to me," he calls. "I'll catch you. It's not far, Hannah. You have to try."

"I *am* trying." I wrap my arms around my chest.

I inhale and focus. It is quiet up here.

All I can hear is the wind, which keeps blowing my hair around my face, and the rustling of leaves. The Fens are spread out below, the sky reflecting back at me from glimmering ribbons of water. There is a white bird on the pond to my right – a swan, I think – and a flash of brown that might be an otter. A figure moves on my right, out towards Hockwold, too far away for me to recognise, all dressed in black. Another one of us kids maybe, taking a day off?

I glance at Dylan. His lips are pressed tightly together, as if he wants to say something but doesn't dare. He's trying to be quiet, which isn't natural for him.

Amy is almost directly below me in a circle of roses, her arms still folded and her foot tapping impatiently. She probably doesn't care what happens to me.

At the thought, I lurch a little higher.

Crikey, she's right! If I work myself up, I literally work myself *up*.

I tear my eyes from her annoyingly perfect face and look at the Fens again, counting waterbirds.

The wings on my ankles start to flutter more slowly.

I shift to counting clumps of sedge and I don't dare check, but I think the ground is getting closer.

"Hannah."

My name is only a whisper. I tear my eyes from the ground and look sideways. I'm level with Dylan's outstretched hand. "Do you want me to pull you in, or do you want to keep . . . you know?" He jerks his chin towards the ground.

"Pull me in," I whisper back, as if speaking louder will make my power flare again.

I reach out carefully, our fingers touch, and Dylan tugs me towards the Tree. As soon as I can wrap my arms around a branch, I release his hand. Then I haul myself into the heart of the oak and tangle my legs around the trunk, awkwardly righting myself.

The doves fidget angrily on a twig above our heads, but make no further moves to attack.

"That was scary close," Dylan says.

"You're welcome," Amy calls. "*Now* will you go away and let me have my space?"

I climb down the Tree, trying not to get angry, but *honestly*. Dylan follows me down, looking prepared to catch me if I rocket upwards again.

"I've got some bandages in my bag," he says, as my feet hit the ground. "From that time I sprained my wrist. Maybe we could wrap your wings up, it might stop your power from—"

"Where's Dolio?" I ask suddenly. I want to check on my tortoise; they aren't meant to fly and he must be terrified. But he isn't between the roots of the tree. "Dolio?" I start to panic, and my feet lift off the ground.

Dylan's hand slams on to my shoulder. "Oh no, you don't!" He gestures at the ground. "Dolio's a tortoise, he can't have gone far. He's probably chased a butterfly *very slowly* under one of those bushes." He blushes in Amy's direction, then glowers as if he's just remembered he's meant to be annoyed with her. "This is your fault, Amy. You can help us look."

"I don't think—" she starts.

"They're *your* bushes," I snap, kneeling. "Dolio?"

There is no sign of him.

"Dolio?" I crawl through the grass. Dylan joins me and I notice that his shirt is ripped. It must have happened when he caught Dolio.

"What if he's run away because I dropped him?" I gasp. "What if he's gone for ever? Hermes trusted us with his pet and now I've lost him!"

"He's a *tortoise*," Dylan repeats. "You can't have been up there more than five minutes. How far can he have gone?"

We're already quite a way from the Tree. I stop crawling and stand. Amy hasn't moved. She's still perched on the root of the oak, with her arms around her chest.

"Are you going to help us look, or not?" I shout.

Amy shakes her head. Then she pauses. "It's not for the reason you think," she says, finally. "If I come out there and start crawling around, I'll just grow a bunch more bushes. It'll make it even harder to find him."

She has a point. Tears gather in the corners of my eyes. I've been looking after Dolio my whole life – but he did originally belong to Hermes. How can I tell Hermes that I lost him? And what will I do without my tortoise?

CHAPTER FIVE

EVERY TUFT of grass, every thicket of reeds and every pile of rocks looks like a tortoise, when what you want to see is a tortoise.

There is no sign of Dolio.

"I don't understand it. How has he gone so *far*?" Dylan moans as he searches inside a clump of reeds.

I sit back on my heels and wipe my eyes. "What if he's been taken by an . . . an eagle?" I wail. "They eat tortoises."

Amy snorts from behind us. "An eagle? Really, Hannah?" She bats a dove away and it flutters plumply upwards, only to return to circling her head like some kind of misshapen moon.

I sniff. "All right, what about one of *them*?" I point at a swan. It eyes me suspiciously, then plops into the water where it becomes instantly majestic.

"Swans don't eat tortoises," Amy says.

"So you're an ornithological expert all of a sudden, just because you have *doves*?" I stop and turn in a circle. "He's run away, hasn't he?" I glare at Amy. "And it's *your* fault! Why couldn't you just leave us alone?"

She flushes.

"Hannah, don't—" Dylan starts, and I'm about to ask why when I spy a black-clad figure running towards us. I think it's the same one I saw from above the tree.

"Hey! Guys?"

For a moment I can't work out who it is, then I frown. "Is that Alastair?"

Dylan sighs. "Oh, *great!*"

A black and white bird is fluttering alongside him. A magpie. For a moment, all I can think of is the old human rhyme: *One for sorrow, two for joy, three for a girl, four for a boy, five for silver, six for gold, seven for a secret never to be told . . .*

One magpie. That stands for *sorrow*. A horrible omen. Does it mean I'll never get Dolio back?

"Guys? Wait!"

The magpie alights on a low tree branch and Alastair keeps jogging along the path towards us. I force the rhyme from my mind and wince. Alastair isn't the last person I want to see right now (that would be Zack Prince), but he's *definitely* in the bottom five. He's the class weird kid, and I'm talking here about a class containing kids who can fly, spontaneously create strawberry laces and shoot lightning bolts from their fingers.

He's always been a bit strange, but a few months ago he went kind of goth, dyed his mousy curls black and started to wear lipstick. Now his belly jiggles over his too-tight black jeans, a black long-sleeved T-shirt with a pentagram on it declaims that he is 'sick of summer' and a spiked choker with a Victorian-looking silver locket dangles around his throat.

He is sweating so much that his curls are sticking to his forehead and his eyeliner is running. He's holding something in his right hand. Something brown and hard and . . .

"Dolio!" I sprint towards Alastair with my arms held out. My power coughs a little and I start bouncing as I did earlier, great steps that are half-flight. My wings pump above my socks.

Dylan runs after me. "Careful, Hannah!"

I reach Alastair, and he hands Dolio over. I clasp him to my chest, and I'm sure he looks happy to see me.

"Where did you find him?"

Alastair points vaguely in the direction he'd come from.

"But . . . how did he get all the way over there?" Dylan asks.

Alastair shrugs.

"And why aren't you in school?" Amy demands, coming to join us.

"You aren't in school either!" Alastair says.

"Who cares?" I glare at her. "We're lucky he was here!"

Alastair makes an 'aw shucks' noise as I find a dandelion and pick it for Dolio. Then I put Dolio and the weed together in my bag. After a moment, the sound of munching calms my racing heart.

"There," Amy says, batting away another dove. It flies upwards, then it spots the magpie. As if the magpie is well, *me*, the dove arrows towards it, emitting an oddly aggressive coo. These doves are *mean*! The magpie releases a harsh warble, a bit like a motorbike trying to start, and flutters away.

If you can strut while flying, that is what the dove does on her way back to Amy.

Amy rolls her eyes. "You've got your stupid pet, Hannah – can we go home now?"

I look at her. Amy's shoulders are almost completely coated in poop and there's some clinging to her perfect hair. I catch Dylan's eye. "Fine by me. I don't want to try my wings again without a rope."

"That's fair." Dylan looks at his watch. "It's basically lunchtime anyway. Mum won't be too shocked if I turn up at home. I'll tell her the canteen was out of fries."

The three of us start towards Hockwold-cum-Wilton, Dylan positioning himself strategically between me and Amy. Moments later, Alastair jogs to join us.

"Why *are* you out here, Alastair?" I say.

Unlike the three of us, Alastair doesn't have powers to practice. His family live in Hockwold, but they're kind of honorary residents.

"I just needed a me-day," he says, swinging his arms in that odd way of his. He walks as if he's doing it according to a manual, as if he's read the best way to walk and is determined not to fail some kind of test.

"I guess I can understand that," I say. If we're upset because our powers are rubbish, how must Alastair feel knowing he'll never have powers at all? My wings give a sympathetic flutter.

Dylan shoots out a hand and grabs the strap of my bag. "Keep it chill, Hannah."

I smile gratefully at my best friend. Then my smile drops. Who is Alastair's best friend? I realise that I've never seen him hang out with anyone.

We head through Wilton together, trailing cooing doves and roses like the tail of a comet. A throaty chirrup from a bush shows me the magpie has decided to come with us too, perhaps hoping Amy might lose one of the beads in her hair, perhaps wondering what the doves see in us. Or maybe it's waiting for an opportune moment to take revenge on the one that attacked it. I give it a nod of fellow feeling.

An unspoken truce allows Amy and I to walk without argument. We pause only when we reach the Hockwold border.

"Home again, home again . . ." Amy whispers.

"You guys," Dylan says, frowning. "Where's the marker stone?"

"What?" I turn. How had I missed it? There is a space where the stone has always lived. A patch of mud on the edge of the path, square and empty. "But . . ."

"Maybe the council moved it?" Amy suggests, and Dylan smiles at her as if she's said the cleverest thing.

"Yes. Maybe it needed . . . cleaning?" Alastair agrees. He waves his hand over the empty spot as if he thinks it more likely that the stone has turned invisible.

"It shouldn't matter, should it?" I say. "I mean, it was only a stone, a focus for the magic; the barrier spell is cast from the temple, right?" I fix my gaze on the green and step across the border.

There is no electric shock, and nothing changes. The cross in the centre of the green hasn't elongated into a sword.

I raise my eyes. In front of me, I can see Hockwold Hall. My eyes widen. "Dylan!"

He steps towards me, tensing as he does every time he passes across the boundary. Then he frowns.

"No shock, right?" I say in a small voice.

Dylan points at Hockwold Hall. "It's . . ."

"Hockwold Hall," I whisper.

"What are you two going on about?" Amy strides forward, then stumbles. "What's happening?"

Alastair is the last to cross the invisible line. He stands next to Dylan, shaking his head and blinking as if there's a problem with his eyes.

Then he takes a deep breath. "OK, you guys. OK . . . i-it's not a problem. They probably just . . . moved the barrier. Right? That's all. We just need to take a few more steps. They were probably going to tell us tonight at dinner . . . or at school. That's right. We all missed Assembly, didn't we?"

I nod and so do Dylan and Amy.

"Well then, everyone else must know what's going on." Alastair squares his shoulders. "I mean, thank Prometheus we didn't come back later – I bet they'd have been here watching us and laughing." He laughs, a strange hiccupping sound. "We just have to keep walking until we find the new boundary."

"But why would they—?" Amy starts.

Dylan takes one of my hands. Wordlessly, I reach out with the other and Amy hesitates before taking hold. Alastair snatches at Amy's fingers. She wrinkles her nose but leaves her palm in his. We take a breath and creep forward in a reluctant human chain.

One step, two steps. No electric shock.

This time I'm watching Hockwold Hall. I think we all are.

Three steps, four.

"How far did they move the boundary?" Amy laughs, nervously.

Five steps, six.

The four of us burst into a run. We run until we're standing right in front of Hockwold Hall, with its brick gables and clusters of chimneys. It doesn't transform into a palace of soaring columns and glittering marble. It remains stubbornly Elizabethan.

Dylan is gripping my hand like he's falling off a cliff. Amy's nails are digging into my palm.

"They wouldn't have shifted it this far," I say, eventually. "They just wouldn't."

"Hannah's right," Amy says. "No *way* Zack's dad would allow the hall to sit outside the barrier."

"What does this mean?" Alastair asks.

I look at him, my skin turning cold and clammy. "I don't know exactly. But one thing I do know – if there's no barrier, then ordinary humans can get in and out of Hockwold . . . and who knows what they'll see. We'll be overrun in no time, with news vans and scientists and tourists. We have to warn everyone!"

CHAPTER SIX

AMY PULLS her hand out of mine and wipes it on her dress like I've given her germs.

"I don't care what *you're* doing," she says. "I'm going to find Mum. I'm going home."

Quickly, Dylan takes his own hand out of mine. "Shouldn't we stick together?"

"What for?" Amy marches away from us, and her doves follow. The magpie hops closer, as if trying to see what the fuss is about. *One for sorrow.* Steadfastly, I ignore it.

"Let her go, Dylan." I shrug. "Her and her flying vermin."

Alastair shoves his hands under his armpits, as if he doesn't know what to do with them. "I-I want to go home too."

Dylan nods, and so we split up, heading for our own front doors.

Only, it isn't my front door, which has, until now, been a welcoming archway; it's an ordinary human door. It is, in fact, blue. There's a brass knocker.

I try to push it open but to my surprise, it's locked. We never lock our doors in Hockwold. What would be the point?

Frowning at the bell, I press it with my thumb. There is a distant muffled ringing: an out of tune, cringey piece of vaguely familiar classical music played through a speaker on the other side of the wall. After a moment, I see a shape behind the frosted glass and the door opens.

Mum is balancing Henry on her hip. He's got hold of her hair with one fist and is waving a toy car in the other one. She steps back and frowns.

"Hannah? Why aren't you in school?"

"Mum," I sag, relieved. "What's happening?"

"What do you mean 'what's happening'? What's happening, young lady, is you seem to be bunking off school! Your father will be furious! And what's happened to your *nose*?"

"But the barrier . . ." I step into the hall.

There are family photos on the walls.

Before I'd left this morning, there had been pictures of me in my first toga, Henry at his formal presentation to Zeus, Mum and Dad's wedding at the temple, that sort of thing.

Now there's an image of Dad playing cricket (as far as I know, Dad has never played cricket in his life). There's a photo of Mum selling cakes at a fair on the green, a picture of me at . . . is that a *preschool graduation*? The wedding photo is still there, but it's changed. Now Mum and Dad are standing in front of St James's church in Wilton.

What's going on?

"Mum . . ." my voice trembles. "I'm sorry I skipped school today, but I got my powers."

"Your *what*?" Mum frowns. "Is this some kind of game, Hannah? Did that awful boy skip school today too?"

"Dylan was with me." I sigh. "And Amy, and Alastair."

"Amy *Fairchild*?" She looks surprised when I nod. "Well!" She puts her free hand on her other hip. "I can't say I'm impressed with any of you."

I march past her, remove my bag, and drop it in the hallway. Then I take Dolio out and carry him to the kitchen.

Something has happened here too. It's an ordinary human kitchen now, like you might see in a brochure. Where is the family hearth? The bread oven? Mum's cauldron?

At least the Coco Pops are in the usual place, and the milk. I find a bowl, locate a spoon and sit. Then I put Dolio on the table beside me. The table has an Ikea sticker. Dolio looks as shocked as I am.

"Mum," I say. "Are you going to tell me what's going on?"

She starts to make herself a cup of tea. I notice she uses a teabag, with no sign of her dried herbs.

"I don't know what you mean, dear."

"All of *this*." I gesture with my spoon. "Where's the hearth?"

I sit up straighter. "Where's Grandad's staff?"

"His what?"

"His staff, Mum, his *staff*!"

I abandon my half-eaten cereal, leap to my feet and race into the living room. Henry tries to grab my hair as I pass. Fortunately, he's not that agile yet.

When I enter the living room, I skid to a stop. Everything here has changed too. There's even a flatscreen TV! To be fair, I've always wanted one of those, but it's wrong. All wrong. It's all too *human*.

Hermes' staff, however, is hanging in its usual spot, looking out of place above a padded sofa. It's a four-foot-long winged rod, intertwined with two snakes doing something I'd rather not look too closely at, and carvings of the other gods.

I shudder in relief and point. "His staff, Mum!"

She appears in the doorway behind me. "That old stick?"

"That. Old. Stick?" I gape at her. "The '*don't touch it whatever you do, that's your grandad's and contains a lot of power*' old stick, you mean?"

She frowns at me. "I know it's your grandad's, Hannah. I wish we could get rid of the thing, but you know what your dad's like. History, ancestry, blah, blah, blah."

I stare at her, speechless.

I stare some more.

"Mum . . ." I clear my throat. "Um . . . what was your day like? I mean, you woke up and then . . .?"

"Hannah, you're acting very strangely." She pulls a baby bouncer out from behind the sofa and plops Henry inside. He babbles happily.

"I know." I force a smile. "Just . . . humour me, OK?"

Mum sighs. "OK then. Henry woke up. I fed him and had a shower. Your dad left his magnifying glass on the table in the spare bedroom and, while I was dressing, the sun caught it and it caused a small fire. You know – you were there."

"A . . . magnifying glass?"

"Yes." She looks at me like I've hit my head. "The one he uses for his hobbies. The sun came through the open curtains, caught the glass and burnt a hole in the table. I had to get the fire extinguisher. Are you all right, Hannah?"

I swallow. "Then what, Mum?"

"You went to school, or *so I thought*." She glowers. "I got Henry dressed. We went to a council meeting. Very dull. Mr Prince wants to put speed bumps around the school and on the high street."

"Speed bumps?" I echo. "Nothing about greater involvement in human politics?"

"*Human* politics? Hannah, you're being very silly. No, it was speed bumps. I came back here to feed Henry his lunch, your dad said he was going to stay out and count the cars on School Lane, to support the council's proposal, and then you came in. I'm worried about you." She reaches over and puts her wrist against my forehead and shakes her head. "At least you aren't running a temperature."

"There's nothing wrong with me." Although my nose does ache. Then my eyes widen. "Great-grandmother's urn. Is it still—"

"In the spare room. Why wouldn't it be?"

Mum follows me upstairs as I race to check.

"OK," I exhale, shakily. "We've still got the urn and Grandad's staff, but everything else has changed." I look at her and my lip wobbles. "*You've* changed, Mum."

"Hannah, I—"

"You really don't remember anything else from this morning? Dad trying another spell?"

"Now you're being *ridiculous*." Mum folds her arms and I take a step backwards. Mum's great, but when she gets annoyed . . . "Go to your room, do some homework and I'll make lunch. Then I'll have to call the school to apologise for your absence this morning. If this is what the teenage years are going to be like, *well . . .!*" She flounces out of the room and down the stairs. "If you need me, I'll be sending a few emails."

"Emails!" I gape.

Herman Messenger's wife sending an *email*. As far as my parents have always been concerned, emails, much like text messages, are the work of Hades.

My power coughs and I fling out a hand to grab the door handle, but I only lurch a few centimetres above the ground and then land again, hard.

"Don't jump on the landing," Mum yells. She sticks her head out from the living room. "Honestly, Hannah. I don't know what's wrong with you today! *And take that dirty animal off the kitchen table!*"

"Yes, Mum."

I take the stairs two at a time. Dolio has two feet in my cereal bowl, and he's happily nibbling on soggy Coco Pops.

"At least *you're* cheerful," I say, as I pick him up and wipe his feet with a tea towel. "Mum's sending emails . . . we have to get out of here."

I sneak out of the back door before Mum can send me to my room again, and sprint to the corner of the street. My feet barely lift off the ground.

I meet Dylan coming the other way. "It's a nightmare," he gasps, holding one hand to a stitch in his side. "I got home and there they were – Susan and Derek Vine. A psychiatrist and a home brew enthusiast. He collects beer mats!"

I shake my head in disbelief. "Mum is sending *emails*."

"It's the apocalypse," Dylan says.

"I don't know what it is, but it must be something to do with the broken barrier." I shake my head. "Instead of making Hockwold *look* ordinary and human, whoever moved the stone has somehow made Hockwold *actually* ordinary and human."

"They didn't even know who they *were*." Dylan is almost crying.

"I know." I put an arm around him, and Dolio nibbles his ear comfortingly. "Why aren't we affected though? I remember who I am, and you know who you are, right?"

Dylan jerks his ear away from Dolio (I guess being nibbled by a tortoise isn't that comforting after all) and thinks for a minute. "Whatever it was, maybe it only affected everyone *inside* the barrier. We were outside when whatever it was happened."

"So, *we're* OK, but everyone else is . . ."

"Human!"

"There's something else." I pull down one of my socks and turn my winged ankle towards him. "Do my wings look smaller to you?"

Dylan crouches, frowning. "I'm not sure. Should they?"

"I've been pretty stressed, but I haven't shot skywards once since we got back."

Dylan's eyes widen and his hands fly to his shirt pocket. He removes a bunch of strawberry laces. Then, we watch his pocket. Slowly, the missing laces regenerate. Very slowly.

"Our powers are weakening," Dylan says, his face turning pale.

CHAPTER SEVEN

"**WHAT ABOUT** your . . . you know?" I point to my own ears.

Dylan closes his eyes and tilts his head, listening. Then he reopens them. "I've still got a connection to the underworld, but it's faint." He swallows. "The others need to know. I'll get Alastair." He starts towards the end of the road, then turns back. "You get Amy!" He begins to run before I can suggest we swap.

I know he's right and we should stick together, it's just that Amy is the most annoying creature since Cerberus (Hades' three-headed guard dog) had puppies.

I reach her front door and am not really surprised to see that it's pink. In the front garden is a tall tree with a platform on it, like a pirate's lookout. I hammer the knocker and, moments later, Amy opens it.

"Ssshh!" She holds a finger to her lips. "Mum went for a lie down."

"She doesn't know who she is, does she?"

Amy shakes her head and, for a moment, she looks upset. Then she looks down her nose at me. "I'm sure everything is going to be fine."

Above her head there is only a single dove, and it doesn't seem that bothered, if I'm honest. In fact, it seems to be wondering what it's doing here.

"Amy," I whisper. "Have you noticed?" I point upwards. "Your powers are weakening."

Amy smiles – a proper, wide smile – the kind I don't think I've ever seen on her face before.

I mean, of course she smiles, when she's made a joke at my expense, or that time Dylan tripped over his laces and dropped his lunch on Zane. And she often wears a sort of half-smirk that says: 'I'm better than you and I know it'. But seeing *this* smile makes me realise I've never actually seen her truly happy.

"I know," she says. "You'd better come in."

I follow her into her living room. I've never been inside Amy's house before, but the place must have been made more human, just like mine. Where there ought to be a family hearth, there is now a decorative mantelpiece topped by a portrait of her mum (although, knowing how vain Amy's mum is, that might not have changed). There's an enormous TV in one corner and, in the other, a stereo system with huge speakers. Above it is a dusty old picture showing an unusual image of Aphrodite, holding a sword instead of her apple and standing with two other gods. I squint.

"Is that Aphrodite with Dionysus and Hermes?"

In the picture, Dionysus (Dylan's great-grandfather) wears the usual vines around his head and wields his familiar pitcher of wine but, less usually, he has snakes at his feet and a ghostly figure by his side. Hermes, my grandfather, is grinning with a frankly evil expression and holding a terrified cow under one arm. It's not the usual image people see of him, but it actually fits the impression I have of him – what with him having been a thief and general troublemaker since before I was born.

"What?" Amy turns. "Oh, that old thing. Yeah, Mum usually covers it up – it embarrasses her. I mean, those two are the least cool gods there are. No offence."

I sniff, to show that I am offended. The picture doesn't fit with the room, and I wonder why it hasn't been turned human like everything else.

"Amy, are you OK?" I ask when she sits down.

"I am, actually." She smiles again. It's creeping me out. "It's going to take me a while to get used to 'New Mum', but honestly, this is good. In fact, it's great!"

"Great?" I stare at her. "My mother is sending *emails*, Amy!"

"And?" She shakes her head. "Hannah, you spent half the morning upside down, in midair. If I hadn't been there, who knows where you'd have ended up!"

I open my mouth to deny that she was any help, but when I realise I can't, I scowl at her instead.

She keeps talking. "Zack can shoot lightning from his fingers. You know how much of a bully he is. Do you think that's going to end well for Dylan?"

"No, but—"

"If this carries on, I'll be able to go places without having to worry about growing roses. And I'm down to one dozy dove." She looks up at it, almost affectionately. "I can be *normal*, Hannah."

"What's so great about being normal?" I glower.

"It wouldn't matter to *you*." Amy rolls her eyes. "You're lucky."

"Lucky?" I lurch to my feet.

"Yes, lucky!" Amy stands to face me. "You think I *like* having to play Helen every time our teacher does the Trojan War? Or having to *kiss* Zack in *every single* play?" She mimes sticking her fingers in her throat. "Or the fact that no one has ever bothered giving me a grade on anything. Ever!"

I frown.

"That's right! Did you know that I only ever get a tick, Hannah?" She waves her arms. "It doesn't matter if I've tried my hardest – I get a tick. I can hand in a blank piece of paper, and I get a tick. I can write a dumb limerick on a maths problem and get a *tick*."

"That doesn't sound so—"

"Are you *kidding*?" Amy stares. "No one expects anything of me, except to be *pretty*. If my skirt has a spot of mud on it, they'll say something. If I haven't styled my hair, they'll comment. But if I don't bother to do any work . . . Well, that's OK, Amy Fairchild doesn't need brains anyway! Can you imagine trying your hardest and no one even bothering to read your work, because what's the point?"

"I—"

"You think it's so terrible, being you?" Amy is panting now.

She shoves a finger into my chest, and I stumble backwards. "You have *no idea*. What do people expect of *you*, Hannah Messenger? I'm expected to grow up beautiful, fall in love with Zack Prince and have pretty, powerful babies!"

She shudders.

"I don't know what you're intending to do about all *this*," she flings out a hand, "or even if there is anything you can do. But whatever you're planning, count me out. I'm *pleased* this has happened. I'm *happy* my powers are going. I'm *delighted* that I've suddenly got a mum who might actually want me to do well at school and then date someone with more going for him than the ability to shoot lightning from his fingers."

She stops to catch her breath and I stare at her, for a moment lost for words.

"I had no idea."

"Why would you?"

I bite my lip. "I thought you had it so easy."

She looks down at her feet.

"You're always so *mean*," I say, eventually.

Amy fidgets. "I know. I-I'm . . . jealous of you," she whispers.

I gape at her. "You're *jealous*? Of *me*?"

"No one makes any demands of you. You can go out in yesterday's clothes if you want. You just hang around with Dylan—"

"Dylan?"

She shrugs. "He seems fun."

"He is." I swallow, then I take her hand. "You know that no one makes any demands of me because no one ever sees me, right? I got my powers this morning. My parents didn't even notice. You got a pizza party for your gift day. I got told off for being too noisy."

She blinks at me. "I guess . . . I guess we're both invisible, in our own way. When people look at me all they see is what they want to see . . ."

"And they don't see me at all," I finish.

She squeezes my hand. "But I still don't want to fix this. I can't help you, Hannah. I'm sorry."

"I understand." And I do. I let her hand go. "At least the objects of power don't seem to be affected."

She frowns at me. Even when she is frowning, she is still pretty. "What do you mean?"

"Grandad's staff and Hera's urn were right where I left them this morning."

Amy turns and points. "If that's true, then where is Aphrodite's apple?"

"What?" My gaze follows her arm. I hadn't noticed the display case under the picture of her mum. It's a glass box, with a broken gold lock.

And it's empty.

CHAPTER EIGHT

"**I'M STILL** not helping you!" Amy gasps as we run. "It's just that . . . well, it's *Aphrodite's apple*!"

"I know."

"The damage that someone could do!"

"I *know*." My side hurts and, even though I only got my powers this morning, I'm already missing my ability to run super-fast.

"It started the *Trojan War*, Hannah!"

"*I know!*"

A single dove flutters above us. Dolio is looking speculatively at it from my bag as if wondering whether it would taste as nice as a butterfly.

We race into my garden and barge through my back door. Amy hesitates, perhaps thinking it would be polite to shout a greeting to Mum first, but I leg it straight into the living room.

There's a bare patch on the wall.

The staff is gone!

"*Mum!*" My voice shakes.

"Hannah, is that you?" Mum appears at the top of the stairs with a half-naked Henry in her arms. He grins at me and waves. "I'm changing Henry . . . Why aren't you in your room?"

"Mum, did you move Grandad's staff? Get rid of it, like you said you wanted to?"

"Don't be daft, Hannah! I've been busy. Hello, Amy." She smiles. "It's lovely to see you. You look very nice today." She frowns a little at Amy's head. "You know you have a little something . . ."

"She has bird poop in her hair, Mum." I stamp a foot. "It's not important. Did you move the staff, or not?"

"Of course not." She shakes her head. "You're being very rude, Hannah, I—"

I grab Amy's hand and drag her towards the door. "Got to go, Mum. I'm doing a school project with Amy."

As I open the front door, Henry babbles as if he's trying to tell me something.

"Hannah," Mum shouts. "I forgot to tell you, your friend came over—"

I slam the door and lean on it.

"The staff is *gone*." Even though I'm not hungry, I feel empty. "If it's fallen into the wrong hands . . ."

"Hermes is just a messenger," Amy says with a toss of her hair. "His staff basically makes him go fast. How much damage could it do, really?"

I stare at her. "Hermes wasn't a messenger because he was *fast*, it was because he could go *literally* anywhere. *Anywhere*, Amy! That staff can open the borders between the living and the dead."

"Oh . . . That's why your dad's the one trusted to call Hera back, because of the staff?"

I nod.

"Ah." Amy bites her lip. "What if what's happened – everyone turning human, I mean – what if someone did it to us, so that they could take the objects of power without anyone trying to stop them?"

I clutch my stomach. "I feel sick. There's a reason all that power was spread out between the gods. If it was held by only one being, they'd be . . ."

"Stronger than Zeus," Amy whispers.

Dylan is waiting for us on the green with Alastair. He's leaning on the cross and nibbling strawberry laces like a nervous tic, and Alastair is shuffling from one foot to the other. Alastair looks up as we arrive. His nose is red, as if he's been crying. It doesn't match the recent goth transformation.

"Mum can't remember a thing," he says. "She thinks she's related to some athlete. There's a picture of him carrying the Olympic torch, above the altar in the hallway."

"Our objects of power are missing," Amy snaps, ignoring him. "Dylan, where's your family's spear?"

Alastair gasps and Dylan turns pale. "Hermes' staff has gone?"

"It was there when I got home," I say, "but not when we checked just now. Aphrodite's apple has vanished too."

"Holy. Hecking. Hades." Dylan's eyes widen. "I have to go home."

Together, the four of us race across the green towards Dylan's house.

There aren't many people around, but those that are here are behaving eerily human: they're gardening, unloading supermarket bags from cars, pushing babies in prams, talking on mobile phones. It's not that we didn't do those things before, exactly, but I mean – who would bother weeding without a bit of magic?

Only Gwyn Hunter from the big house on the end pays us any attention. He opens his mouth, no doubt to ask us what we're doing home in the middle of the day.

I raise a hand. "School project . . ."

He doesn't have a chance to answer before we're sprinting past.

Amy runs alongside me with grace and elegance, despite the dove that keeps getting in her way. Alastair pants behind us and, even though my pigeon wings give me a bit of a boost, Dylan pulls ahead and hits his front door first.

"Wait for us!" Alastair calls, but Dylan vanishes upstairs.

Ignoring her irritated coos, we shut the dove outside and stand in the hallway awkwardly, until Dylan comes back down looking relieved. "It's still there."

"Where?" Alastair says.

"In its hiding place." Dylan leans on the wall. "We don't put the spear on display. Someone took it out of its case at Dad's birthday party a few years ago, thinking it would be fun to get everyone drunk. The spear makes people lose all their inhibitions though, so it makes you *super* drunk and *super* embarrassing. Not cool."

"So, it's safe then?" Alastair says.

Dylan nods.

His mum appears from the kitchen. She has Dylan's red hair and lanky build, and is wearing an apron.

"Dylan, you didn't tell me you were bringing friends over!"

"Sorry, Mum, we aren't staying." Dylan herds us towards the door.

I wave. "Bye, Mrs Vine."

"Bye, Hannah, darling!"

"Right," I say, when we reach the corner. In the garden next to us, Mrs Hunter is mowing her lawn. I lower my voice. "We're going to have to check on the other objects of—"

Amy's elbow connects with my gut and knocks the breath right out of me. I double over until I can inhale again, then rocket back up with a mouthful of insults ready to hurl.

Then I see the two humans.

They're standing in front of us, taking photographs of Hockwold Hall. They're wearing hiking trousers and rucksacks with dangling water bottles, sunglasses – even though it's not that sunny – and peaked caps.

Dylan is staring, his mouth open. "They're . . . they're . . ."

"Don't say it," Amy hisses.

"But . . . they're not *allowed*!" Dylan wails.

The lead human, a man with a paunch and a teeny-tiny beard, spins around.

'Not *allowed*?" he snaps. "Not allowed to *take photographs*? This is a public space. What's more, we're considering booking the hall for our daughter's wedding."

I look from the human to the front door of Hockwold Hall. "You're considering what for the who now?"

The other human, a woman, turns around, spots the dove flying above Amy's head and squeals. "Thomas, *look*!" She turns her gaze to Amy. "You have *trained doves*? That would be perfect for the wedding! Where are your parents?"

"You can't have your wedding here," Dylan says.

"Rubbish!" The woman cries. "Hockwold Hall is a Former Royal Residence." She takes a leaflet out of her pocket and begins to read aloud. "The historic hall is surrounded by manicured lawns and gardens . . . wood-panelled walls, open fireplaces, a grand staircase. It sounds lovely." She turns to her husband. "Do you think they'll let us in to look around, Thomas?"

Thomas gives us a little glare and nods. "Of course they will. It's a business." Then they march right up to the front door and ring the bell.

As I watch, still barely able to believe what is happening, Zack's mum opens the door. They speak for a moment, then she gestures them inside.

"But . . . but . . ." Dylan says.

"At least there's nothing magical for them to actually see," I say.

"But they don't *belong* here," he wails.

Alastair shrugs. "Maybe they do now," he says.

CHAPTER NINE

OVER AT St Peter's church (formerly the temple dedicated to Zeus) another human has appeared. This one is doing the strangest thing. He has stuck a large sheet of paper over one of the graves and is rubbing a crayon over the stone.

"What do you think that's about?" Amy whispers.

I shrug.

The magpie – I'm assuming the same one from earlier, although there could be a whole flock of them appearing one at a time, just to annoy me – lands on the church wall in a flurry of wings, and the human turns and spots us.

"Kids! *Kids!*" he waves a hand. I look at Dylan, but don't see how we can avoid going to speak to him.

We drag our feet across the road.

"Are you locals?" he says excitedly. "Do you know much about the history of the church?"

I shake my head. "We're not really into that kind of stuff."

"Oh." The man looks disappointed. "So, you don't attend the church here?"

"Not *that* church," Amy says. She's right, we attend temple when Zeus commands it, but not this human version. "We're more into . . . older stuff." Amy winks at me.

"Paganism?" The man blinks up at us through his glasses. "How interesting."

"*Hardly*," I snap. "If you must know . . . the Greek gods. They were first, after all."

The man snickers. "Well, if you believe that . . ."

"What?" Dylan bristles.

The man stretches and stands. "I don't mean to offend you. I love the Greek gods – and the stories always cheered me up, you know? Persephone and Hades, Theseus and the Minotaur, Perseus and the Gorgon . . . Icarus flying too close to the sun, King Midas and his golden touch. Heroes, villains, monsters – those stories have it all. In fact, I'm a bit of an expert on world religions. If you'd really like to know—"

Alastair leans forward. "*I* would!"

"Alastair!" Amy hisses, as he puts his elbows on the wall as if preparing for a lecture. His locket swings over the front of his T-shirt. It looks old and expensive, and I try to remember if he used to wear it before he went goth, or if it's as new as his T-shirt and hair dye.

The man smiles. "Well, before the Greek gods were the Titans."

"We know *that*," Amy says. "And *they* weren't gods! Completely different thing."

"All right," the man laughs. "But before the Titans—"

"There wasn't anything before the Titans," Dylan says.

The man shakes his head. "That's where you're wrong. Where do you think the Titans came from?"

I frown. "I . . . I hadn't thought about it. No one's mentioned it. I mean, in school we get taught about the war between the Greek gods and the Titans."

"Yeah," Dylan says. "When the gods won dominion over all the worlds, living and dead."

"You were taught that in the local primary school? How impressive." The man wipes his glasses. "I'd love to chat to your teacher." He looks around as if Miss Wisdom is going to pop up from behind the wall. Then he frowns and looks at his watch. "Hang on a moment, shouldn't you be in sch—"

Dylan grabs my arm. "Leg it!" he cries, and we run towards the green.

Amy tugs at Alastair and he follows more reluctantly. "I thought that was interesting," he says, as we round the corner and lean on the wall outside the council offices. "What do you think he meant about beings older than the Titans?"

"He doesn't know what he's talking about," I say. "He's just a stupid human and *we* need to focus."

"Right," Dylan says. "So, who stole the objects of power?"

"And are there any more missing?" I add. "There are nine items in Hockwold, right?" I tick them off on my fingers. "The thunderbolt, the apple, the spear, the staff, the shield, the hammer, the trident, the arrow and the quiver. We know the apple and the staff have gone, and the spear is safe. What about the thunderbolt and all the rest?"

"I didn't think of that!" Dylan looks alarmed. "You think Zeus's thunderbolt—"

There's a burbling coo from above our heads. Amy's dove is dizzy and exhausted. To be fair, she has been flying in circles all morning. I touch the scab on my nose, reminding myself not to feel sorry for the feathery assassin.

Amy raises her arm. "Come on, Myrtle." The dove drops on to her wrist and nuzzles Amy's palm. It glowers at me, and then at the magpie which is fluffing its feathers on the wall over the road, then settles down to sleep.

"Myrtle?" Alastair says.

Amy narrows her eyes at him. "Hannah's stupid tortoise is called *Dolio*! At least Myrtle is a real name." She turns to look at Dylan, but he's pressed himself against the wall, as if hiding from someone on the street.

"Dylan, what . . .?"

"Zack and Zane," he mutters, frowning at his melted footwear. "What are they doing out of school?"

I peer around the corner. He's right, Zack and Zane are heading towards us. I can hear them laughing.

"*They're* bunking off school now too?" Alastair says.

"Just what we need!" I roll my eyes. "If we want to find out if Zeus's thunderbolt has been taken too, we have to go to Hockwold Hall. There's no way to avoid running into them."

CHAPTER TEN

HOCKWOLD HALL has a curved driveway. We wait until Zack and Zane have vanished into the house and then creep along it, keeping close to the bushes.

"It's not like we're planning to break in," Amy says after a moment, and she starts striding off ahead.

"Yes, but . . ." Dylan watches her go. "That means we'll get there faster," he mutters. Alastair nods and fingers his locket. Amy, however, is already ringing the bell.

It tolls with a much classier *ding-dong* than the tune welcoming visitors to my house.

We crowd behind Amy. Me first, then Dylan and Alastair at the back

Zack opens the door. He's had time to change into a Nike tracksuit and is eating an apple. He gapes at Amy, and I see his chewed-up mouthful. Then he glares past her at the rest of us.

"What are you losers doing here? And where've *you* been all morning, Ames?"

Amy gasps. "That's not *Aphrodite's* apple, is it?"

Zack tosses his half-eaten core out of the door and on to the lawn behind us. Amy almost faints. I peer at the core (which is gross, as it's just been in Zack's mouth).

"It's OK," I tell her. "It's just an ordinary apple."

She groans in relief.

"Well," Zack says. "What do you weirdos want? And why are *you* with them, Amy?"

I hadn't thought this through. "We ... um ... I ..."

Amy rolls her eyes. "I don't want to do what I'm about to do," she mutters to me. "I'm trying to get away from all this."

Zack narrows his eyes. "What did you say? Away from all what?"

Amy tosses her hair and her curls bounce on her shoulders. She smiles at him. "I don't know why *they're* here, Zack, but *I* thought we could go for a walk."

"A walk?" Zack's eyes light up.

"Yes, to the park." Amy offers him the hand that hasn't got a dove perched on it.

"To the park?" he echoes. "Wouldn't you rather stay here?" Zack points to a room behind him. "We've got a new Xbox game. We told Miss Wisdom we weren't feeling well, so we've got all afternoon to play."

Amy shakes her head and casts me a meaningful glance. "I was hoping we could hang out without your brother, Zack." She turns, heads around us, and strolls back up the drive. "Or do I need to ask *Dylan* to come with me instead?"

Zack rushes out of the door, shoving past as if we aren't even there. He reaches Amy and puts an arm around her shoulder. "What are you carrying a bird for?" he says, as they turn the corner.

Dylan and Alastair look at me, then at the open door, and we rush inside.

"All right," I whisper. "We need to be quiet and avoid *that* room." As I point, there's a loud explosion and a yell, and I jump, wings fluttering. I hover for a moment and then bump back to the floor.

Nothing else happens, but another shout comes from behind the closed door. Zane will be in the games room, as long as the explosions keep coming.

"I don't think we need to worry too much about being quiet," Alastair says, and Dylan grins.

"OK," I nod. "Where do we think Zack's dad would keep Zeus's thunderbolt? We just need to check that super-fast, and then we can leave."

"Dining room," Alastair says. "Above the table."

We look at him.

"We were invited for dinner a few weeks ago," he says. Then he flushes. "I know the gods generally don't think much of my family, what with the whole 'stealing fire' thing, but Mr Prince wanted Mum's vote for the new human-relations bill, so . . . dinner."

Dylan claps him on the shoulder. "Lead on."

We tiptoe down the hall and into a dining room with a huge

table and twelve chairs upholstered in velvet. There's a portrait of the whole family looking smug on one wall, which almost makes me vomit, and on the other wall there are . . . two empty hooks.

"*There*, above the table?" Dylan points at the empty space.

I sink into one of the chairs, barely even noticing how comfortable it is. "This is so bad."

Alastair nods.

Dylan sits beside me and puts his head in his hands. "If the thunderbolt is gone, then should we assume all the other objects have been taken too?" He looks up. "Dionysus's spear is safe because it's hidden, but everything else was kept on display."

I groan. "We can't waste time trying to get into half the houses in Hockwold just to check."

"Then what are we going to do?" Dylan pauses. "And how did Dolio get in there?"

Dolio is sitting in the middle of a huge vase of flowers, chewing industriously. I pick him up. He stretches his neck to keep chewing, so I reach across, pull out a bunch of very expensive looking stems and stuff them in my bag. He climbs over me to get back in with them.

Dylan shakes his head. "We aren't equipped to deal with this. We need a grown-up. I vote we tell Zack's dad what's going on."

Alastair swallows. "Are you sure that's a good idea?"

I leap to my feet. "No way, Dylan! If he thinks he's human he won't believe us, and if he doesn't think he's human . . ." I tail off.

"What?" Dylan stares at me.

"Well, if he knows who he really is, that means he must have

HANNAH MESSENGER

been outside the barrier when the spell happened. Which means he's likely the bad guy."

Dylan points at the empty wall. "Would the thunderbolt be missing if he was the bad guy?"

I bite my lip. "That could just mean he's keeping the objects together."

Alastair leans on the table. "This is hurting my head."

"I just . . . I think we can do this ourselves." I look at Dylan and Alastair. "I mean, don't you want to fix this without anyone's help? Don't you want to be . . . a *hero*?"

Dolio sticks his head out of my bag just as a sharp knock at the window makes me turn. The magpie is pecking the glass with its beak.

Alastair jumps.

"Why is that thing following us?" I snap. "Is it after Dolio?"

Suddenly there's a commotion from the hallway and the sound of voices.

"Let's get out of here," I say. "We'll be in trouble if they find us. If Mr Prince *has* lost his memory, who knows what he'll think of a bunch of kids being in his dining room. And if he *hasn't*, we can't let him know that we know . . ."

"Yes, all right." Dylan is already racing for the window. He tries to open it, but it's stuck tight. "We can't get out this way."

"Into the hall!" Alastair cries.

I run for the door and stick my head out. Zack's parents are in the hallway, speaking to the two humans we saw earlier.

"A May wedding would be lovely!" Mrs Prince is saying. "I'm

61

not sure what you mean about the doves, though."

Mr Prince is built like a professional wrestler. He's big and booming and takes up so much space that it's almost difficult to see the others by the door. His dad is Zeus's last son: Yiannis Kouros, born in Greece in the nineteen-fifties. The humans don't officially *know* Yiannis is a demi-god, but they *know* in their hearts he is differemt. They call him 'The Running God'.

I slip into the hallway, with the boys right behind me. Unfortunately, I have no idea where to go next. I look at Alastair and give him a 'what now?' face.

He looks panicked.

"Back door?" Dylan hisses, and Alastair points. But getting to the back door means going past the games room where, at any moment, Zane could stop blowing things up on the Xbox.

Suddenly, I spot Dolio heading for a vase of flowers sitting on a table at the bottom of the stairs. "Dolio!" I hiss.

I dart after him and bend to pick him up, just as the Princes are saying their goodbyes. As I close my fingers around his dusty shell, I notice the tablecloth sweeping the floor. I slide underneath, scooting until I touch the back legs.

Seconds later, Dylan scrambles in after me, then Alastair, who, just as the front door closes, rearranges the cloth so that it hangs evenly and covers us all.

"I thought you were caught for sure then, when Mrs Prince turned around," Alastair whispers. "She looked right at you."

"She can't have done," I say with a frown.

"She did," Dylan agrees. "Right at your legs."

I clutch Dolio to my chest as the Princes head upstairs. The treads vibrate under Mr Prince's weight and the table shudders as if in sympathy.

Then a door closes above us, and, explosions aside, the house is quiet. Alastair takes a deep breath and peers out from under the cloth. "All clear!"

We crawl out and run for the door. Which opens right in front of us.

CHAPTER ELEVEN

"**WHAT ARE** you lot doing in my house?" Zack is standing in the doorway, Amy right behind him. She makes frantic faces at me but, honestly, I have no idea what she's trying to communicate.

"Nothing!" Dylan pushes past, knocking Zack out of the way. I rush out under one of his arms and Alastair follows. We hit the driveway running.

Behind us I hear Zack speaking to Amy. "Can you believe those losers!"

"Absolutely not!" Amy says. "Thanks for the walk, Zack. Sorry, about those thorns cutting your ankle. I've got to go!"

She races after us.

We reconvene on the village green and sit under the cross that ought to be a sword. The shadow falls across my face and the magpie, *one for sorrow*, lands on a lamp post at the edge of the grass. Why is that thing still here? I put Dolio safely in the bag and look away from it.

"Was Zeus's thunderbolt there?" Amy whispers.

I shake my head. "No. We have to assume that whoever is behind this has taken all the objects in Hockwold, except Dylan's spear." I rub my head. "But who could be doing this?"

"Well," Alastair is sitting slightly apart from the group, leaning against the stone plinth. "*Hermes* is kind of known for this sort of thing."

I leap to my feet. "I *knew* that would come up at some point. Stuff goes missing, and it must be Hermes!"

"He *is* a trickster," Alastair says. "And he's not in Hockwold."

"Neither are a lot of the gods," I snap. "There's only Zeus, Poseidon and Demeter behind the gate right now, and Hephaestus living on the outskirts of town."

We all glance at the big metal gate across the green, and away again.

"Hermes is imprisoned in Tartarus," Dylan says. He looks at me. "He *is*, right? I mean, we'd have heard if they'd let him out . . ."

"For the last twenty years," I snap, still glaring at Alastair. "And anyway, I don't think *any* of the gods would steal their own stuff. I mean, why would they?"

Alastair spreads his hands. "To become more powerful."

"But *why*?" Dylan shakes his head. "Everyone's happy in Hockwold . . . aren't they?"

Amy shrugs and Alastair looks away. I realise that Dylan is dead wrong. Not everyone is happy in Hockwold.

"All right then," I rub my eyes and lean on the cross. "What about an enemy of the gods?"

"What enemy?" Dylan says. "The Titans are locked up, deeper than Hermes, and guarded by some seriously scary dudes. Who else is there?"

Amy frowns. "What was that human saying about where the Titans came from?"

"He didn't know what he was talking about," Dylan says. He looks at me. "That's right, isn't it, Hannah? If something older than the gods was around, we'd have been told."

I nod. "They're always warning us about the Titans. '*Never trust a Titan*'. Even Prometheus gets a bad rep and Zeus agrees humans would have died out ages ago if he hadn't nicked fire for them. If there was a bigger bad out there, they'd hardly keep it a secret."

Alastair wraps his fist around his locket and holds it to his throat. "You think it has to be someone from Hockwold, don't you? One of the gods' descendants. One of our parents or their friends."

I think for a moment and then I nod. "Yeah, I do," I say. "The gods wouldn't do this; if they wanted to be even more powerful, they wouldn't have retired. Humans outside Hockwold don't even know we exist. So that only leaves someone from here."

Amy looks thoughtful. "What about Hades?"

I look at her. "What do you mean?"

"He never retired, did he? What if *he* wants more power? I mean, historically he's been a bit . . . testy."

Dylan shakes his head. "Only when people try to escape the underworld." He twists a finger in his ear. "I think I'd have heard if there were rumblings about Hades. One of the grannies would have said something."

Amy gets to her feet. "We'd better tell Zeus what's going on."

Dylan jumps up. "No way! When Dad interrupted one of Zeus's chess games, Zeus hit him so hard with a thunderbolt he couldn't sit down for a *month*."

Amy looks to me for support. "Zeus won't mind being disturbed for something *this* important."

I glance across the green, towards the metal gate that we'd have to go through to get to Zeus.

Behind the gate an avenue is lined with trees that cast deep and twisting shadows over statues of the big twelve, which are rumoured to come to life and do horrible things to visitors without appointments. The gate is very much locked and there is no welcome mat big enough to make it look appealing.

'I really don't want to face Zeus,' Dylan says. 'What if he decides this is our fault, somehow?'

I swallow. "I think I have an idea. I know how we can catch the thief."

Alastair brightens. "Then we *don't* have to visit Zeus?"

I bite my lip and look at Dylan. "You aren't going to like it."

Dylan doesn't just dislike my plan. He *hates* it.

"You want to set a trap, using my spear, the only object of power that is safely hidden? Not a chance!"

"I think it's a great idea," Alastair says, clapping me on the shoulder.

"We can protect the spear, Dylan," I say. "All we need to do is parade it around the village, so the thief knows we have it. After that, we watch to see who comes to steal it. Then we've got them."

"But then they'll have the spear!" Dylan points out.

"That's what you think," I say.

CHAPTER TWELVE

WE WAIT for Dylan on his garden wall. Amy is stroking Myrtle, I'm feeding some leaves to Dolio and Alastair is kicking his heels against the bricks. The horrible magpie seems to have decided we are the most interesting thing in the village and is hanging around in a tree at the end of the street. Just in case it's decided to try a new diet of tortoise, I shift to shield Dolio from its stare.

Finally, Dylan emerges from his house, dragging his feet and looking miserable. He's wearing gloves and carrying a spear as tall as he is. Weirdly, it is tipped with a pinecone.

Alastair jumps off the wall and reaches out a hand. "Is that . . ."

"Be careful," Dylan puts the spear behind him. "You don't want to get drunk."

"Doesn't it create wine too?" Amy asks.

"Yes," Dylan sighs. "Along with water and milk. It's also very pointy, so keep back." He hands me the fishing line I'd asked him to pick up and looks at me. "Now what?"

I put the line in my pocket, jump off the wall and hold out a hand to help Amy down. "Now we parade up and down the village, so the thief can see us with it."

"I hate this," Dylan says.

I pat his shoulder. "It'll be all right," I say. "What could go wrong?"

We set off, with Dylan leading. He's holding the spear in front of him, as if it's going to bite.

The weirdness does gain us some attention.

"What are you kids doing?" Mr Hunter shouts from his doorstep.

"Taking this stick for a walk, Mr Hunter," Alastair shouts, and Amy giggles.

We turn the corner that leads to Hockwold Hall and Dylan freezes. I almost stride into the back of him. Zack and Zane are outside eating ice cream.

Dylan retreats but it's too late – Zack has spotted us and his eyes light up. He marches right for us, Zane scrambling to catch up.

Zack flicks his blonde hair and frowns at Amy, then at me and Alastair, then at Dylan. "Give it," he says, holding out a hand.

Dylan stares. "Give what?"

"The cool spear." He gestures. "Hand it over."

Dylan backs up.

"Give it," Zack says. "Now!"

Amy steps between them. "Why do you want it, Zack? Do you know what it is?"

Zack shrugs. "I know it's too cool for those losers. So, give it here." He lunges around Amy and Dylan leaps sideways, tripping over the kerb and rolling to protect the spear. As Zack bends forward to wrestle it from him, still holding his ice cream, Dylan reels away.

Zack gestures and Zane steps up. "Just give it to him, Dylan," he says. "It's not a big deal. You can always make another one, can't you?"

"There are two of us and only one of you," Zack crows.

"Actually," Alastair says in a shaking voice, "there's not just one of him." He poses in front of Dylan, holding up his fists like a boxer. His hands tremble and there is a sheen of sweat on his forehead. "There're *two of him*. Of us, I mean."

"Three, actually," I say, putting my hands on my hips. I glance meaningfully at Amy, and she rolls her eyes. Myrtle is resting on her shoulder and I'm sure the dove rolls her eyes too. But then Amy moves to stand next to me. We form a line between Zack and Zane, and Dylan.

"Four," she says, with a sigh.

Zack gapes at her. "What are you doing, Amy? You're my girlfriend."

"Gross!" I mutter.

Dylan regains his feet and puts the spear behind his back.

Amy winces. "Look, Zack, I never actually agreed to be your girlfriend. I think we're too young, and anyway, I . . . I don't like you that way."

71

Zack looks as if Amy has punched him in the face. "Course you do," he says, running his hand through his hair.

"I don't, I'm sorry," she says. "I don't want to hurt your feelings but—"

"You like *Dylan* now, is that it?" He sneers. "You and the biggest loser in school. You know what that makes you?"

"Does it make me a loser?" Amy asks, and Myrtle coos.

"A great big loser," Zack yells. "Wait and see how popular you are when I'm through with you."

"That's not nice!" Alastair shouts, and he swings a fist. It isn't a particularly hard swing, and his aim is terrible, but he manages to nudge Zack's elbow. Zack's arm flies up and he hits himself in the face with a splat of chocolate ice cream.

We all stare as the mess runs down his nose and chin. Alastair retreats a step.

After a moment, Zane touches his arm. "Zack?"

Zack is shaking with fury. Dolio pops his head out of my bag. He looks at me, then at the road, then at me again.

"Dylan," I murmur. "Dolio's right. We should run."

We turn and sprint towards the school as if Cerberus has come to town and we've nicked his favourite bone.

CHAPTER THIRTEEN

A FURIOUS YELL from behind tells me that we can't slow down. Dylan is out in front, the spear held over his head. Amy and Alastair are right behind me.

My bag bangs against my back and I hope that Dolio isn't feeling too sick, what with all the jolting.

We turn the corner to see the school directly ahead. Dylan stumbles and I almost crash into him. But then I freeze, seeing what Dylan has: my dad is standing on the pavement, clipboard in hand, making notes.

Amy bangs into me and gasps. Then she sees Dad too. "What's he *doing*?"

"Mum said he was counting cars." I swallow.

"Alastair Ignatius! You *pathetic deadbeat*!" Zack yells and, without hesitation, Alastair sprints towards my dad.

Dad's eyes widen at the sight of us. I am running just behind the terrified Alastair and Dylan is holding the spear in front of him like it's a pooping baby. Amy is right behind us with her dove now flying overhead.

I look back. Zack and Zane Prince have almost caught up. Zack has ice cream dribbling down his face and neck.

Dad almost drops his clipboard. Then he strides towards us, glasses glinting, sunshine highlighting the scorched curls in his hair and moustache.

"Zack Prince," he snaps, in a voice I don't think I've ever heard him use. "That's enough!"

Zack and Zane stumble to a stop, centimetres from Alastair.

Zack opens his mouth.

"I don't care!" Dad says, before he can speak. "Go home before I call your mother."

The brothers look at one another, and Zane catches Zack's arm. "We'll get him another time," he says, and Zack nods. Then they start back the way we'd come.

I try to sidle past but, for a change, Dad does in fact notice me. "Hannah, what is going on?" He raises his clipboard. "These roads aren't safe. Why are you running around like a bunch of wild dogs? And why aren't you in school?"

Alastair leans closer to him. "Mr Messenger, do you know what that is?" He points at Dylan's spear, and Dad shrugs.

"Dylan's stuck a pinecone on a stick. Very creative." He looks at the school behind him and then sighs. "I ought to make you go to class, Hannah," he says. But then he winks. "But I can't say I never took a day off. Go home, kids. And stay away from Zack Prince."

A car turns the corner and Dad gasps. "Now you've made me miss a tally," he snaps, and places a mark on his notepad.

"Thanks, Dad!" I shout, as we head back towards the green. I look at Alastair. "Why did you ask Dad that question?"

Alastair shrugs. "We've got to suspect *everybody*, haven't we?"

"Not my *dad*!"

Amy exhales. "That was close." She looks at Alastair. His eyeliner has completely rubbed off and his lipstick has faded to a grey smudge. "Thanks for sticking up for me, by the way."

Alastair blushes. "It's fine."

She looks as if she wants to say something else to him, but instead she turns to me. "Do you think we've drawn enough attention?"

Dylan gives a tired groan. "I think I'm through parading now."

I peer around us. "I can't see anyone following us, can you? No one looking particularly interested in the spear?"

Amy turns and walks backwards. "No one," she says. She almost wobbles into Dylan, who leaps away from her, holding the spear over his head.

"*Careful!*" he yells.

A sparrow lands on the pinecone at the end of the spear and pecks at it. Dylan shakes his arm, trying to dislodge it. The spear glows, and the bird flutters off the end. It flies around in a circle, a little like Myrtle with Amy, then it weaves left, then right, tweets, hits a tree and drops to the ground.

Amy gasps. "W-what happened?"

Dylan shakes the spear. "One touch of the end of the spear,

Amy, that's what I've been trying to say."

Amy backs away from him and the spear. "So, if Zack had got hold of it . . ."

"It would have been bad," I say, taking her arm. "Come on. Your mum will still be asleep, won't she?"

We stand in Amy's garden and I point at the tree I'd spotted earlier, with its pirate platform.

"I haven't been up there in *years*," Amy says. "I don't even know if it's safe."

"It looks all right to me." I turn to Dylan. "So, what we need to do is, use the spear to make the ground at the bottom of the tree boggy. Like *really* boggy, so that if anyone walks into it they'll be stuck."

"*That's* your plan?" Dylan says.

"Then we tie *this* fishing line," I remove it from my pocket, "to the spear. Lay it in the middle of the boggy bit and hide on the platform. When the thief comes to steal the spear, we pull it up to safety. Then, while they're stuck in the bog, we get them to tell us where the marker stones and all the objects are hidden and how we change everyone back. We can threaten them with the spear."

I mean, it should have worked.

CHAPTER FOURTEEN

DYLAN TOUCHES the spear to the earth beneath the tree and mud starts to bubble as if it's hot. Then milk gushes up from under the roots. It smells slightly sour and immediately starts to soak into the ground.

"I've just got one question, you guys," Alastair says, as the scent fills the garden. "If we just leave the spear out here lying around, won't the thief *know* it's a trap?"

"Not at all," I say. "The reason being, the thief doesn't know that we know who we are. Or that we know that they know who they are."

Alastair moves his lips as if he's trying to work out what I just said.

"As far as the thief is aware," I say, "we just found this old thing in Dylan's house and now we're bored of playing with it."

"What if they saw us making the bog?" Amy says, turning

around. But the street is empty of everything except our shadow: the magpie. It lands on the wall opposite and tilts its head at the ground. I glare at it. Maybe if we give it one of Amy's shiny hair beads, it'll go away.

"I still think this is too big a risk," Dylan says, lifting the spear back up. The ground in front of him is sodden.

"Trust me, Dylan." I hand him the fishing line. "My grandad's the trickster, isn't he? So, I know a good trick when I make one. Remember the bucket of gravel and the trampoline?"

"That got us detention for a week," Dylan grumbles.

"It worked though, didn't it? Tie this on."

Dylan sighs and ties the line to the spear. It is very nearly invisible. You'd have to know it was there. I grin.

"How's the bog, Alastair?"

Alastair pokes a stick into it. There's a sucking noise, the stick disappears, and he jumps back. "It worked! It's just like the Fens."

"Course it did. Go ahead, Dylan." I point. "Place the bait."

Dylan looks unhappily at me. "You're really sure about this, Hannah?" He looks at Amy. "What do you think?"

Amy rubs her elbows. "It *should* work."

Dylan bites his lip for a moment longer, then he weighs the spear and carefully tosses it into the roots of the tree. It lands sideways on, rolls a little towards the bog, then lies still, the fishing line shimmering slightly between the end of the spear and Dylan's closed fist.

"It looks brilliant," Amy says, and Alastair nods.

"Quick," I say. "Up the tree."

I run for the wooden ladder which is nailed to the back of the trunk, and am halfway up, with Amy and Dylan behind me, when I look down. Alastair hasn't moved.

"Come on, Alastair!"

He shakes his head, looking paler even than usual. Then he drags his fingers through his curls. "I-I can't, Hannah."

"What do you mean, you *can't*?" I hiss.

"I-I'm scared of heights."

I really can't think of a way to get him up the tree, and we don't have time to muck about. "Can you see another hiding place?"

Alastair looks around. "Maybe."

"Well, *find* somewhere." I wring the rung holding me high above him. "The thief could turn up at any moment!"

"All right!" He turns and runs out of sight.

I keep climbing, until I reach a trapdoor with a weathered handle. I push it up and clamber through on to the platform. It's built among the leaves and branches of the tree, high above the road. In one corner, there is a little chair, a pile of mildewed Lego and a Barbie with a spiky haircut and a mouldy boilersuit.

I wonder if we can be seen from the ground and hope we're well hidden.

Amy pops her head through the hole in the floor. She frowns. "Hannah, where are you?"

"I'm right here!" I say, and she rubs her eyes.

"There you are! Were you always this good at hiding?" She pulls herself up on to her knees and thrusts her hand back down to catch Dylan's.

"I wasn't hiding," I mumble, as Amy pulls Dylan on to the wooden boards.

"Hey, is that car-mechanic Barbie?" Dylan sniggers, as he spots the toys. Amy picks her up and stares at the doll, misty-eyed.

"She was . . . what I was never allowed to be," she says.

"A mechanic?" Dylan frowns.

Amy shakes her head. "A mess." She shrugs and puts the doll down.

Dylan looks confused.

"Have you still got hold of the spear?" I ask, squinting to see the transparent line running from his hand.

Dylan nods. We all slither to the edge of the platform and lie flat.

"I don't remember it being this high," Amy whispers.

Below us the spear looks small as a matchstick.

"I hope Alastair's OK," Dylan mutters.

I try to spot him, but there's no sign. "He's found somewhere to hide," I say. "And it's probably a good idea to have someone on the ground. Just in case . . ."

Dylan doesn't look impressed with that 'just in case', but he doesn't say anything.

After a while, Dolio crawls out of my bag and sits on the platform beside us. Myrtle hops over and perches on his shell. He glares up at her, but it makes no difference, she just fluffs out her feathers and settles. He turns his baleful glare on me, and I shrug. "Sorry, Dolio."

Time ticks on. The spear lies there, doing nothing. Trees sway in the breeze. A cat stalks around the tree and vanishes under a bush.

"How *long*?" Amy groans. "School will be finished soon."

"The thief *must* have seen us with it," I say.

"You'd think." Even Dylan seems tired of looking down. He rolls on to his back. His fingers fall next to Amy's, but she doesn't move her hand. In fact, her fingers twitch until their little fingers are touching. Just barely, but she has to know it.

I narrow my eyes. What exactly is going on here? Dylan is *my* best friend.

Then I remember the spear is more important and fix my gaze back on it. Where is the thief?

Suddenly, Dylan sits up, rubbing his head. "The ghosts are *yelling* at me. But it's really distant, I can barely hear them." Then he frowns. "What's that smell? Holy Hecking Hades – is that *smoke*?"

I feel a gentle thud; Dolio is back in my bag. I clamber on to my knees. Dylan is right, my eyes are stinging.

"How can it be smoke?" Amy is rubbing her eyes too.

I scoot towards the trapdoor, but only get halfway before the boards under my palms grow warm. I draw as close to the trapdoor as I dare and that's when I see an orange flicker. The ladder is on fire. As the rungs turn to ash, flames lick hungrily at the platform and start to eat through the dry wood. My heart pounds, and my mouth goes dry.

"Grab something!" I yell, no longer caring who might hear. "The platform's on fire!"

"*What?*" Amy shrieks, and throws her arms around the branch above her. Myrtle flutters up to sit beside her.

As Dylan reaches for a handhold, the board beneath him groans and cracks in two. "*Dylan!*" I scream.

CHAPTER FIFTEEN

MY **HEART** leaps into my throat, but Dylan doesn't fall. At the very last moment, he catches hold of a branch and ends up dangling above the burning floorboard.

He turns a horrified expression in my direction. I'm sitting near the centre of the burning platform, with no handholds within reach. There is only one branch above me, but I can't get to it.

I scramble to my feet and stretch. Leaves flutter just above my fingertips. Fire hisses below and the platform creaks and cracks. The wood beneath me begins to blacken.

"Alastair!" Amy starts screaming. "*Alastair, help!*"

The tree itself starts to groan. Once the fire has eaten the platform it will start on the trunk and branches. We're in real trouble.

With a final *boom*, the board beneath me shatters. I jump, knowing I'm not going to make it to the branch.

But then my power gives a familiar hiccup, my wings start to flutter, and I wobble upwards, until my fingers brush bark. As soon as the tree takes my weight, my wings stop fluttering. Now I'm dangling above what is swiftly turning into an inferno. I start to cough.

Amy is still screaming for Alastair. Dylan grips his branch, wide-eyed, his red hair standing out in stark contrast to the paleness of his skin.

Finally, I hear Alastair's voice. "Hannah! Amy! Dylan! What in the name of *Prometheus*! What do I do?"

Clinging to her branch, Amy leans down. "Alastair, there's a metal ladder round the back of the house. If you get it, we can climb down!"

"Ladder . . . right." His voice fades as he runs.

My legs are getting hot now. I can see grass between shreds of wooden floorboard and gusts of smoke. I can't see the spear though, or the bog where we left it, my eyes are too filled with soot. My hands start to ache.

Amy sobs. "I don't know how much longer I can hold on."

"Don't you dare let go," I say. "You hold on as long as you have to."

Dylan laughs wildly. "At least there's a bog below us. We'll have a soft landing."

Finally, I see movement underneath me. "*Alastair?*"

"I'm here." There's a bang as he leans the metal ladder against the tree, right below Amy. "Is that OK, can you reach it?"

Amy reaches out a leg and presses her foot against a rung, then she releases her branch with one hand and grips the top of the ladder. The ladder teeters and settles, then finally she lets go of the branch altogether and shifts her weight across.

"I'm holding it," Alastair yells.

Amy climbs down, leaves catching in her hair as if the tree wants her to remain.

As soon as she is out of sight, Dylan swings his feet on to the rungs and releases his own branch. Then he stops. "You can't reach the ladder from there, Hannah."

"I'll be OK," I say. I look down and swallow. "Go on. I'll be right behind you."

Flakes of ash are making his hair grey, like he's an old man. Dylan hesitates, but then Amy shouts his name, and he starts to descend.

Dylan is right, I can't reach the ladder from where I am hanging. They could move it closer to me once Dylan's hit the ground, but a metal ladder thrust through fire to reach me will get hot. Really hot. I swallow again. There *is* one way down: I could fly. But my power isn't reliable right now. Not even close. It's only boosted me a few centimetres at a time since the barrier came down.

Tears crawl into the corners of my eyes, but the heat burns them away.

I already know that I have to remain calm to control my power, but how do I find calm when I'm hanging off a burning tree?

I hear more noise below. Adults, I think, coming to see what the commotion is. Sounds of panic. I can't hold on any longer.

Sending up a prayer to Hera, and wishing I had a Zen master to help me, I let myself drop.

I plunge through the flames so quickly they barely touch me, and I reach for my power. Nothing happens. I scream and then, as the ground rushes up to meet me, my wings start to flutter.

A beat before I hit the ground, air cushions me and I thump on to my feet, windmilling my arms and losing my balance. A black-clad arm snakes out and steadies me. I grip it, peering up into Alastair's face. He looks bleak.

Amy slaps smouldering ash from my shoulders and hair. Then we stagger out from under the burning tree, blackened leaves floating around us like it's the end of the world.

Dylan is standing in front of the bog, the fishing line slack in his hands.

The spear is gone.

CHAPTER
SIXTEEN

"**W**HAT WERE you kids *doing* up there?"

There's a small crowd of adults grouped around Amy's front garden. Their expressions range from anger to concern.

"I've called the fire department," says a voice.

"Where's your mum?" asks another.

Amy takes a trembling step towards me. "Mum's inside," she says, and someone goes to knock on the door. I don't pay attention. I am staring at the empty spot where Dionysus's spear is meant to be.

"They must have got it when I went for the ladder," Alastair says. "I should have stayed, kept watch. It was obviously a diversion."

"Someone snuck up and set the wooden ladder on fire, so they could steal the spear?" I whisper. Of course they did. "But . . . how did they avoid the bog? And the fishing line?"

"The heat dried out the bog," Amy says. "And it looks like they cut the line."

I try to take Dylan's hand, but he yanks it out of my grip.

"Don't!" he snaps, and he stalks off down the street.

"Dylan," I call after him, "we'll get it back!"

He whips back around, his cheeks flushed. "How, Hannah? How will we get it back? We don't even know who has it!"

One of the adults tries to stop him leaving, but he pushes past and breaks into a run.

Amy sniffs and rubs her wrist across her face. "We should have gone to Zeus," she says.

Alastair clears his throat. "Shouldn't we go after Dylan?"

Amy looks back at her house, where her mum is answering the door, looking sleepy and shocked and very beautiful. The adults crowd around her, immediately forgetting that we are there.

I catch Amy's elbow. "Speak to your mum later." I start down the road, pulling her after me. "If you stay, you'll be stuck here for hours."

"OK." Amy starts to move of her own accord. "Where would Dylan have gone?"

"I know where he is," I say.

Dylan is back on the green, sitting under the cross, with his knees pulled up to his chin.

"Hi." I sit next to him. He doesn't look at me.

Amy and Alastair settle on his other side.

"I can't believe this," he says eventually. "I just can't."

"I know. I messed up." I look at my hands. "We need help. Should we try and get to Zeus?" I look reluctantly at the big metal gate on the other side of the road.

Alastair clears his throat. "If Zeus is still Zeus, and he hasn't been turned human along with everyone else, wouldn't he have done something about this mess already?"

Amy rubs her eyes. "You're saying there's no point trying to speak to him," she says.

I groan. "But we do need help."

Alastair blushes. "I think we *should* speak to one of the gods, just . . . one of the gods who was outside the barrier when all this happened."

"Who?" I say. "Dionysus is in Mexico, remember? Aphrodite's in Paris, Ares in Afghanistan . . ."

Alastair fidgets. "Hermes isn't far away. We know he can't have had anything to do with the theft and—"

"Are you *serious*?" I put a hand on Dolio's shell.

Abruptly Dylan nods. "Alastair's right, Hannah. We can get to Hermes and be back in a couple of hours."

"He's in *jail*, Dylan!" I shout.

"We can break him out," Alastair says, confidently. "I believe in us."

Amy looks hopeful. "There's another advantage to getting help from Hermes."

I raise my eyebrows. "What's that?"

"Set a thief to catch a thief," she says.

Cambridge Castle, or rather Cambridge County Gaol and House of Correction, was closed in 1900. Or so people think. The gods turned it into the entranceway to their own prison, soon after they arrived. It's far enough away from Hockwold so the gods' enemies aren't on their doorstep, but near enough that they can visit and gloat, or throw someone else inside, whenever they're in the mood. Also, it's thematic, which gods love.

We get the bus.

At four o'clock we're standing in front of it. Myrtle is on Amy's shoulder, and she has a rucksack full of torches and batteries that Dylan liberated from his house. I've got Dolio and what feels like half an allotment in my bag, Dylan has a plastic carrier of steaks and Alastair is carrying a bag of what he calls 'prison-breaking equipment', which he seems to have nicked from someone's shed. We all look and smell as if we've been in a fire and Dylan isn't really speaking to me. We got some funny looks from the driver on the Number Forty bus.

There's a rustle, and suddenly Dolio is not only out of the bag but halfway across the enormous, manicured lawn. "How did he . . .?" Amy says. Then she shakes her head. "Never mind."

I run to catch Dolio up and put him back in my bag. "All right, all right. I know you miss him," I mutter.

"I don't think we're meant to be here," Alastair whispers.

"Of course we aren't meant to be here!" I snap. "It's a prison."

"I mean, there isn't anyone here." He gestures. "I thought there'd be like . . . I don't know, a visitor centre. Or guards."

"There *are* guards," Dylan says grimly.

"Have *you* ever visited?" Amy asks, catching up to me and linking her arm through mine. I lean into her gratefully.

"Once – when I was younger. That's how I know how to get inside. Mum went away for the weekend and Dad brought me. She went nuts when she found out, and we haven't been back since."

"I'm sorry," Amy says.

I shrug. "It's OK. I can't miss someone I only met once. It's just . . . when Mum and Dad do notice me, it's because he's the mirror they're holding up to me."

Amy frowns. "I don't understand."

"All my life, it's been '*don't end up like your grandfather, Hannah.*' If I drop a plate, it's not because my hands were slippery, it's because I'm '*turning out like Hermes*'. When they do pay attention to me, it's only because they're checking I'm not taking after him. To them, everything I do is because I'm . . . mini-Hermes. I don't really know him though, so how do I know which bits of me aren't *me* at all?" I sigh. "It's complicated."

Amy squeezes my arm. "You're not Hermes, Hannah. Any more than I'm Aphrodite, or Dylan's Dionysus. I hate the way I look, Dylan is hardly the world's biggest party animal and the last time Miss Wisdom asked you to take a message to the headmistress you dropped it in the nearest bin."

I find myself smiling. "Well, the message did say that Dylan and I had detention."

"You're *you*, Hannah," Amy says, and I nod, my shoulders relaxing.

I wouldn't tell her, but ever since Alastair persuaded us to come and get Hermes, I've been worrying that he'd look and act just like me and prove Mum right. But I have to stop dragging my heels.

We arrive at the front entrance of the castle and I start to look for the hidden gap in the hedge. It's a little way further along than I remember and it takes me a moment to locate it, but once I do, it leads us into the garden, just where I expected.

Cambridge Castle looks a little like Hockwold Hall, if a glazier had forgotten to stop putting in windows. There are hundreds, each with a cell behind it, and I feel as if they all contain eyes, watching me.

"Is he inside?" Amy points to one of the windows and I shake my head.

"No, the entrance to Tartarus is *underneath* the Castle."

Her eyes widen slightly.

"What did he do, exactly?" Alastair asks in a lowered voice. "Hermes, I mean."

"I don't want to talk about it." Alastair doesn't drop his gaze, so I sigh. "Let's just say he played a prank involving Hera's underwear … and a polar bear."

That breaks Dylan's self-imposed silence. "A polar bear!"

"He can go *anywhere*, remember?" I say with a sigh. "I think he got it from Edinburgh Zoo. Anyway, it's embarrassing. And it gets brought up every time I make a mistake."

"Oh," Alastair says. "Sorry."

I shrug.

"I'm the other way around," Alastair says. "Mum *wants* me to end up like my ancestor. He's a thief too, but he's a hero. Stealing fire from the gods, saving humanity and all that."

I don't answer. It's all right for him if his family is pro-theft, but Hermes is no hero and they'll find out soon enough.

After a moment, Alastair keeps talking. "I'm not a hero though," he murmurs. "I'm just a disappointment."

I swallow a sudden lump in my throat. His mum is disappointed because he's a good kid; mine is disappointed because I'm not. Another time, I might have tried to say something nice, but we've reached two large doors which are set into the ground in a secluded corner of the garden. Ram's horns are etched into the wood, and they are padlocked shut.

"That's the entrance," I say. "Last time I came, we had a key from Zeus, which opened everything. This time . . ."

Alastair gets out a pair of bolt cutters. "On it!"

I stand back, a little impressed, as he kneels in front of the shank, puts the blades in place and strains. His shoulders heave, but nothing happens. Eventually, Dylan takes one handle and Alastair takes the other, and they lean all their weight on the cutters until, with a clank, the padlock springs open.

"All right!" Amy whispers.

We each take a handle and open the hatch, levering the doors until they lie flat on the grass like the wings of a moth.

Before us lies a set of stairs leading into the bowels of the Earth. We have opened them to the light, but it is so dark inside that the sun can only penetrate a few feet. It is as if the gloom is a physical thing, devouring the beams that reach it.

Stepping inside will involve stepping into that pool of darkness.

"*That's* the way into Tartarus?" Amy asks, hoarsely.

I nod. "One of the ways. There are a few entrances dotted around the world, wherever is convenient for the gods. This is the one in England."

Amy opens her bag.

"After you," Alastair says, taking a torch from Amy and handing it to me.

I nod and take the first step.

CHAPTER SEVENTEEN

ONE STEP, two steps, three steps . . .

I clutch the guardrail with one hand, continuing to hold the torch with the other. Its shaft of brightness illuminates only two stairs ahead. I feel blind. I remember this from my last visit to Hermes, although that day we had permission to be here and, of course, Zeus's key, which cast more light.

I steady myself and keep going.

The others behind me take loud breaths as if they're going to step into cold water. Then they follow.

Last time we were here, Dad sang songs as we descended. 'Ten green bottles.' 'A hundred bottles of beer on the wall.' 'The ants go marching.' The key in his hand had glowed comfortingly, and it had all seemed much less creepy. I try to hum, but the darkness muffles my voice like a blanket.

The steps start off like normal stairs but, after the first forty or so, they turn into rough stone. After the first hundred, the stone becomes uneven, slick and damp, and my knuckles ache as I grip the guardrail for dear life. The square of light that connects us to the real world grows small and dim, like a distant chandelier with a dying bulb.

Behind me, Amy is grumbling under her breath. Suddenly, one of the boys lets out a curse and I hear them bump into one another. There's a skidding sound and I tighten my hold on the rail just in time for Dylan to slam into me.

"Sorry," he gasps.

"It's OK." I pat his shoulder. "Just don't let go of the rail."

"How much further?" Amy demands.

"We're about halfway," I say, keeping my voice low. "So don't fall."

After about another fifty steps, the staircase takes a turn and I can no longer see the glow of the entrance. Now the darkness presses around us like the ocean, and my tiny dot of light shows me only one step in front.

"I don't like this," Amy mutters.

"It's a jail for the gods," Alastair replies. "Did you think it was going to be the Hilton?"

"Of course not! But I wasn't expecting *this*."

I had tried to tell them, but I suppose it's hard to describe the way into Tartarus. It's about to get worse too.

The first growl reaches us as the echoes of Amy's complaint ripple away.

"What was that?" She grabs my arm. "Is that . . . the guardian?"

I pat her fingers and the dove on her shoulder coos; a tiny, terrified sound.

"Don't worry, Amy," I say. "I know what to do."

The growling gets louder the further we descend, and then, finally, we reach a landing. No more stairs.

I turn my beam on to a jar of matches which sit on a shelf to my right. I hand the torch to Dylan and reach up to take the jar. Then I unscrew the top and light a match on the sandpaper stuck to the lid. It flares to life. I put the tiny flame against the wall.

For a moment, nothing happens, and I hold my breath, thinking I might have misremembered. Then the waiting tinder catches and one torch flares to life, then another, and another until the whole corridor ahead is lit with a yellow flickering light that bounces from the bronze walls in an almost welcoming glow.

That's when Amy screams.

Remember when I said that Cerberus had puppies . . .

The thing about Cerberus is that he spends *most* of his time in the underworld. But every so often, Hades comes up to see Zeus and he brings his favourite pet with him. Last time that happened, Cerberus met and fell in love with a golden retriever named Dizzy.

Dizzy is the sweetest and, yes, the dizziest dog you've ever seen. Cerberus is a maniacal three-headed killing machine.

Their puppies each have two heads. One is a vicious slavering monster, the other wants to lick you to death. Talk about a split personality.

The puppies were left to guard this gateway to Tartarus, partly because they put a whole new terrifying spin on a game of fetch, and partly because people were starting to complain about the slobber.

The growling and excitable barking emanating from the corridor ahead comes from six heads, a total of three puppies: Ammo, Attila and Elsie.

Amy dives behind Dylan and Alastair jumps behind me. Not his best moment, if I'm honest.

"Dylan," I say, out of the side of my mouth. "Are you ready?"

He hooks a steak out of his bag and throws it at Ammo. Ammo's happy head catches the meat, and his psychotic one immediately tries to tear it away. With Ammo distracted, we are now faced with Attila and Elsie.

Dylan throws a steak to Attila. This time the psycho head gets the meat and the happy head whines.

"Aww," says Amy.

"For Hera's sakes, Amy." I nudge Dylan. He's waving a steak at Elsie, but she's stalking towards us with single-minded intent, saliva dripping from both mouths.

Dylan waves the steak harder. Elsie ignores it. There's a ripping sound from Ammo. His meat has torn in half, but both heads are happily chewing . . . for now.

We take another step backwards and my heels nudge the bottom step. I stop moving. At this rate, Elsie will force us all the way back up the stairs and on to the lawn.

"Dylan, she isn't interested in the steak!" I catch his arm. "What else have you got?"

"Strawberry laces?" He tries waving the meat again.

"I don't think she wants strawberry laces!" Amy squeals.

Dolio climbs out of my pack and, before I know it, he's sitting on the floor between us. Dolio looks at me, then he retracts his head and feet and just sits there.

"Not the best place to take a nap, Dolio." I dart forward to pick him up, but before I can reach him, Alastair steps between us.

"Sorry, Hannah," he says, and he kicks Dolio across the floor.

I shriek as Dolio skids along the corridor. Before he can crunch into a side wall, Elsie scoops him up in her jaws.

"Alastair!" I shout and start running towards Elsie, but Dylan grips my arm.

"Look!"

Elsie is holding Dolio gently. She carries him back, puts him on the ground between my feet and then looks at me as if to say *again*!

"*Dolio!*" I scoop him up.

He thrusts out his beak, looks at me, then back at Elsie.

"You can't be serious?" I say.

Elsie wags her tail.

Dolio retracts again.

"I can't believe this." Gingerly, I toss Dolio along the passage. Elsie races after him and catches him, again, softly. Then she brings him back.

There's a growl from Ammo, and Dylan throws another steak.

This time I bowl Dolio carefully, aiming to the left side of the corridor, and Elsie races after him, her tail wagging so hard I think she might take off.

"Come on," Alastair says, edging forwards.

"I'm not speaking to you," I hiss, but I follow him along the wall. Elsie comes with us, carrying Dolio like he's the most precious thing she has ever seen. Even her terrifying head is grinning with pleasure.

The wall has images carved into it. Amy trails her hand across some of the pictures. "This is the war between the gods and the Titans," she says. "Look, here's the cyclops making Zeus his thunderbolt. And the great battles!"

"That's Prometheus." Alastair points, surprise on his face. "Before he was imprisoned."

I touch another of the scenes; the carved lines feel as if they want to move under my fingers. "This is Zeus, after he won – throwing Chronos into Tartarus." I pull my fingers back.

Dylan is standing still behind us, staring at another scene.

"What is it?" I frown.

"This is . . . before the war," he says, and he reaches out to touch the carving. His fingertips brush the lines and he stiffens, then he jumps back with a gasp. "It's . . . speaking to me."

"It can't be." I stride to his side and touch the images myself. This time they do move, shifting under my touch, and I whip my hand back and stick it under my armpit. "I didn't hear anything."

"I think it's the ghosts," Dylan says. "The dead. They're trying to tell me what the picture means."

"What *does* it mean?" Alastair is standing behind us, clutching his locket in a shaking hand. He looks at me, accusingly. "You said there was nothing older than the gods."

"The ghosts say that it's a picture of Eternal Night," Dylan says, his voice echoing in the chamber. "Goddess of Misery. The primordial. She was first."

"That's just not true," Amy whispers. "Is it?"

Dylan nods and tilts his head, as if listening. "That's what they're saying. Her name is . . . Achlys."

The ground rumbles, and I step away from the pictures. "Dylan, should we . . .?"

"From Achlys came Chaos," he says. "Then Night, Day, Love." He pauses. "Then Earth and Heaven, then the Titans we know: Chronos and the rest."

He blinks. I shiver and then Attila growls.

Dylan throws another steak and we run past all the creepy carvings, refusing to look at them, until our way is blocked by a door.

Only it's locked, and I don't have a key.

CHAPTER EIGHTEEN

"**NOW WHAT?**" Amy cries, and Elsie gives a questioning *woof*.

"Alastair?" I look at him. "You said you had a way through the lock."

Dylan chews on a strawberry lace, shaking his head. "The ghosts say it's Zeus's key or nothing," he says.

Alastair reaches into his back pocket and brings out a roll of cloth.

"You've got the *key*!" Amy exclaims.

"Not *exactly*." Alastair unrolls the material to reveal a set of small, spiked instruments. "Ta-dah!"

"What are those?" Amy frowns.

"Um . . . they're lockpicks." He hands them to me.

"What am I meant to do with these?" I stare at him.

"Pick the lock, of course," he says.

Amy gapes. "Why have you got *lockpicks*?"

Alastair flushes. "Nan bought them for me off the internet a couple of years ago. She thought . . . well, because Prometheus was a thief, I might be good at . . . Anyway, I wasn't."

"Well, *I* don't know how to use them." I try to hand them back.

"Are you sure? Your ancestor was a thief too. *The* thief, really."

"Yes, I know. And remember how that's a bad thing and I'm *not* anything like him!"

Dylan strokes Elsie thoughtfully. She wiggles under his palm. "It's worth a try," he says, eventually. "You could have a hidden talent, Hannah."

"For using *lockpicks*?"

"It's that or go home," Amy says.

I sigh and look at the lock. It's old and, compared to one in a front door, for example, pretty big. I select the largest, pokiest-looking tool in the kit, stick it in the hole and wiggle it around. Nothing happens.

"See!"

I am about to tell Alastair where to stuff his picks when there is a gentle *click*. The pick has caught on something and moved it. I try to open the door, but nothing happens.

"You have to put another one in," Alastair says. "Think about the shape of the key. You're trying to create it with the picks."

I keep hold of the first tool and select the second largest, then I poke that into the lock under the first, moving it around until I feel it press against something and then turn it.

I try not to think about the fact that Alastair was right, and I do seem to be good at this. Great, more proof that I'm nothing more than a mini-Hermes. Mum would *freak*.

Something wet touches my leg and I jump. Elsie's evil head is licking my calf. I freeze, expecting teeth to rip into me at any moment, but Elsie is wagging her tail and holding Dolio, who extends his neck and looks pretty happy, all things considered.

"Dylan . . ." I say with gritted teeth.

"Oh, sorry." He crouches. "Come here, Elsie. Good girl." She turns mournful eyes on me and then goes to Dylan.

"I need three hands for this." Holding the two picks with one hand and, thankful that I have long hair and am used to doing plaits which require more fingers than most people are born with, I select an even smaller tool and insert it under the second one. This time the click comes faster and the door creaks and shifts. I keep all three tools in place.

"Amy?"

Amy grabs the big wooden latch, pushes it down and opens the door. I stumble forward and throw down the picks.

"Told you," Alastair says, with a smug expression.

"Pure luck," I say, refusing to meet his eyes. I shove the picks deep into my pocket, hoping I can forget about them.

We are facing another corridor lit by torches. This one has several open doors along each side of us. There is only one that is closed, and it's right at the end.

"Where are we?" Amy murmurs.

"It's hard to explain," I say. "We're still under Cambridge Castle, but now we're also beneath the underworld. We came down through the three layers of night and past the bronze wall. It's . . . well, it's magic. It's Tartarus."

Alastair nods. "But there should be guards," he says. "Shouldn't there?"

"There weren't any last time," I answer. "Although there was a Titan looking after the puppies."

"You had permission to be here last time," Dylan says.

I shrug and stride forward. Maybe the gods thought a descent in the dark ending with an encounter with Ammo, Attila and Elsie would be enough to deter visitors.

We reach the closed door.

Amy points. There's a bolt holding it shut. Elsie presses against my legs, dripping drool on my shoes. Dolio's little legs are moving, as if he wants to run right through the door.

"OK." I reach up, take a breath, and slide the bolt.

The door opens with a loud creak and there, in the centre of the room, is a boulder. On top of the boulder are two huge chains. Chained to the boulder . . .

"Hi, Grandad," I say.

CHAPTER NINETEEN

HERMES RAISES his head and a smile spreads across his handsome face. "Little Hannah, is that you? You've got so big! What are you doing here? I'd get up, but . . ."

He rattles his chains.

The wings on his ankles are much bigger than mine, bigger than Dad's even, and pure white. They flap in response to his movements. His feet are bare and he's wearing a pair of faded Levi jeans with rips in the knees, held up by a leather belt. He has on an open Hawaiian shirt, a frayed friendship bracelet and a digital watch which, shockingly, is still glowing with the date and time. It's all very nineties. Which makes sense, as he's been down here since then.

He doesn't have a beard, which surprises me. I thought he'd look a lot more like someone who'd spent two decades chained to a rock. I imagined at least a bit of five o'clock shadow, but he's clean shaven and bright-eyed. Only the hair on his head seems to have grown longer, the black curls touching his shoulders when he turns his head.

I touch my own dark hair and bite my lip. I do look like him.

"Who are your friends?" Then he laughs out loud. "Is that *Dolio*? Elsie, put him down, right now!"

Elsie whines.

"*Elsie*," he says, warningly.

She drops Dolio at his feet. I blink and then Dolio is sitting on Hermes' chest, nibbling his chin with his beak.

"How did he . . .?" Amy starts, then she gives up.

"This is Amy," I say, as Hermes nuzzles his tortoise right back.

"I've missed you, buddy," he says to Dolio. "Has Hannah been looking after you?"

"This is Dylan." I push him forward. "And Alastair."

Hermes doesn't pay any attention.

"Grandad," I say. "We need your help."

He twists to meet my eyes. "Where's Herman? Where's your mother? Why are you down here by yourselves? And what have you done to your nose?"

I touch my face. Stupid Myrtle!

"That's why we need you," Dylan says. "Our parents aren't . . . themselves."

Hermes frowns. "What do you mean, 'aren't themselves'? Zeus hasn't gone senile and started transforming everyone, has he? He did love a cow . . ."

Amy gapes at him. "My mother has *not* been turned into a cow!"

"It's worse," I say, lowering my hand. "Everyone's become human."

Hermes frowns. "I don't understand."

"There's something wrong with the barrier," Dylan says. "The marker stone has gone missing and now everyone thinks they're human."

"Dad's counting cars and Mum's sending emails," I whisper.

Hermes jerks. "Wash your mouth out!"

"It's true," Amy says.

"Everyone's lost their powers, or doesn't remember they have them," I say. "And . . . someone has stolen the objects of power."

"They've *what*?" Hermes strains against his chains. "My staff?"

Amy nods. "And Aphrodite's apple, Zeus's thunderbolt, Dionysus's spear and, we assume, everything else."

"You haven't *checked*?" Hermes frowns.

"We didn't want to waste time," I say. "Even if the other objects are still safe, isn't it bad enough that the apple, staff, thunderbolt and spear are gone?"

"You're right," Hermes says. "This is bad. Kids, it's *really* bad."

"We *know*!" I shout. "That's why we're here."

"OK." He thinks for a moment and then he smirks a little. "What does Hera think she is, some bent old grandmother, I bet?"

I open my mouth, then I close it again.

"Don't you know?" Alastair says, looking sympathetic. "Hera's dead."

Hermes freezes. "What? When? *How?*"

"I thought Dad would have told you," I say. "I'm sorry. I guess he was hoping he could bring her back before you had to know."

"Bring her back?" Hermes relaxes. "So, she's not *dead*-dead then? She's just taking a break from her body for a bit."

I nod.

"OK, you'd better get me out of here." He lies back on his boulder and waits.

I turn to Alastair. "Have you still got those bolt cutters?"

After an embarrassing amount of grunting and straining, the boys manage to cut through the chains. Hermes sits, stretches and frowns.

"You shouldn't have been able to do that," he says. "Those chains are linked to the same thing that powers the barrier. If they're weak enough to be broken by a couple of eleven-year-olds with a pair of big scissors—"

"*Bolt cutters!*" Alastair snaps.

"Then, you're right. There really is a problem." He tucks Dolio into the waistband of his jeans and pats Elsie on the heads. "We'd better get out of here before the dragon gets back."

"The *what*?" Amy shrieks, spinning round as if a fire-breathing beast has appeared behind her.

Hermes bursts out laughing. "I'm *kidding*! Elsie and her brothers are the guards. I'm the only prisoner on this level right now and really, all they needed were the chains and the big rock." He looks at it with a hate-filled expression. "I wasn't going anywhere."

"Oh, right. I knew that." Amy relaxes.

"Aphrodite's line?" he says, looking at the dove. "Not known for brains, I'm afraid."

Amy stiffens.

"That wasn't nice, Grandad," I say, quietly.

He looks at me in surprise. "Fair enough." He bows to Amy. "Sorry, kid." Then he holds his hand out for Alastair's bag. "Have you got anything in there that I can use to smash a rock?"

CHAPTER TWENTY

"**I WANT TO** bring Elsie with us." Dylan has his arms folded and is glaring at me. "You've got Dolio, Amy's got Myrtle. Why shouldn't I keep Elsie?"

"She's guarding Tartarus," Amy says. "She's got two heads! How are you even going to get her on the bus?"

Elsie whines and licks Dylan's fingers. He pats her golden head, then ruffles her black one. Elsie grins back and both heads drool happily on his tatty trainers.

"Your mum would go *bananas*!" I say. "She won't even let you have muddy shoes in the house."

Dylan looks at Alastair. "Back me up, mate."

Alastair flushes. "Amy's got a point – how will you get her on the bus?"

"Let *me* worry about that," Dylan says.

I look at Hermes. "Don't *you* have anything to say about this?"

He shrugs. Then he grins at Dylan. "She doesn't fit in down here anyway."

And that is why I am attempting to sneak a two-headed dog on to the Number Forty bus from Cambridge to Hockwold. Dylan's hoodie is over the golden head, mainly because Elsie's black head tried to take off the hand of anyone who tried wrapping it up. Dylan is walking in front, I'm on the right, Amy is on the left and Alastair is at the back, so it's difficult to see that there's a weird lump on the dog. Hermes is refusing to get on the bus at all.

"I'm going to fly home," he says.

"You are *not*!"

I knew this was going to be difficult. But *this* difficult? The driver is already looking at us suspiciously and there's an old lady on the lower deck who hasn't taken her eyes off Elsie. I lower my voice. "The humans will see you. You can't."

"Oh, please." Hermes waves an arm. "I've been flying about since before humans could walk."

"Yes, but not since they got mobile phones!" I hiss.

"What, those old bricky things?" Hermes laughs. "What have they got to do with anything?"

"Oh, Aphrodite's apple!" Amy turns around and pulls her phone out of her pocket. Of course, *Amy* has a mobile. I'm not allowed one till high school. "*This* is a mobile phone, Hermes."

He looks at it, then at Amy, then at me. "So?"

Amy rolls her eyes. Then she pulls up TikTok and records a fifteen-second video of Hermes and the rest of us. She adds a few flourishes. Then she shows it to him.

Hermes gapes.

"*What is that?*"

"That's you," Amy says. "And believe me, if anyone sees you buzzing overhead, you'll be a meme on the internet faster than you can say 'viral'."

"What does any of that mean?" Hermes looks at me. "What did she say?"

"She says if one person sees you, then every single human in the world with one of those phones will be able to see you too."

"But . . . but . . ." Hermes looks horrified. "That's . . . I mean, what a breach of privacy."

"Says the god in prison for stealing Hera's knickers," mutters Dylan.

"Here." Amy waves the phone. "If you get on the bus, I'll show you how to make it play cartoons."

The driver glares at me as I pay for all of us, and we make our way down the aisle.

"Hey." The old woman half stands. "What breed is that dog?"

"She's half golden retriever, half Cer—" Hermes starts.

I elbow him hard in the stomach. "She doesn't like strangers, so you'd better stay back."

"Huh." The old woman sits back down.

"What a cutie," Hermes says, and twinkles his eyes at her.

The bus journey would have been a lot worse without YouTube. Hermes is completely absorbed in *Teen Titans Go* for the entire journey.

Elsie, luckily, is perfectly happy sitting with her black head on Dylan's thigh and gazing at him adoringly. Every so often, a snore comes from under the hoodie. Dolio is sitting on Hermes' lap, as happy as a tortoise can possibly be, and Myrtle is perched on Amy's shoulder watching Elsie nervously.

We pull into Hockwold as the sun is starting to go down. Twilight is turning the sky purple and lengthening the shadows of the trees as we walk Hermes to the bare patch of earth that shows where the marker stone should have been.

Elsie growls. With both heads.

Hermes hisses through his teeth. "This isn't good."

"You didn't believe us!" I straighten indignantly.

He ignores me, then he marches forward. After a few strides, he pauses and looks back. "The barrier really is broken."

I nod and he rubs his chin.

"I'd better—" Hermes starts, and that's when a spike of absolute agony takes me out like a bullet to the brain.

CHAPTER TWENTY-ONE

MY **KNEES** go weak and I grip my head as a whole bunch of weird memories swirl into me. I remember going to Hockwold Primary School with Dylan, Amy, Alastair and all the others. I remember the nativity plays at Christmas – I was usually a sheep – and I remember maths lessons, field trips into the Fens, learning French phrases and reading Biff, Chip and Kipper books. I grip my head.

"Ow! Ow!"

I remember *enjoying* all these lessons. I'm looking forward to going to high school next year. I am particularly excited to be doing all three sciences: biology, chemistry and physics.

"Holy cow." My eyes swim. "I think I'm going to be sick."

I can just make out Dylan's concerned face. "Hannah, are you OK?"

I remember refusing to join Brownies because Dylan couldn't.

I remember going to St Peter's Church on Sundays.

"Aaargh." My head spins.

I remember choosing all my bedroom decorations for my seventh birthday – I was heavily into Pegasus in those days, so flying horses were a big theme.

But now . . . now I also remember another seventh birthday shopping trip, begging for a blue sofa and all of us being pleased about how nice it looked against the pink wall. I remember putting luminous plastic stars on the ceiling. I remember both things.

The new memories are overlaid like a bad bit of photoshop on an existing picture.

I throw up.

Amy shrieks and leaps away from me. "Gross!"

"Are you OK?" Alastair sounds worried.

I sink to my knees and close my eyes. False memories swirl, trying to take over. "You guys . . . I think I'm turning human."

I crack open my eyes to see Amy crouching next to me. "What do you mean?" she says.

"I mean, I'm starting to remember things that I know never happened." I look at Dylan. "This is *freaking me out.*"

Dylan bites his lip. "You mean we're *all* going to lose our memories? Like everyone else. That us knowing who we really are . . . it was only temporary?"

I nod and grab my temples. Elsie leaves Dylan's side and licks my hand. Twice. With each head.

Dylan looks terrified. "We can't lose our memories! I'll *never* get the spear back."

I stand back up, slowly. The memories seem to be settling at different levels, like fruit juices poured into a glass. My brain feels like a stripy cocktail. "What about you guys – how are your heads?"

"I feel OK right now," Amy says. She looks at Dylan. "But we're running out of time, aren't we?"

I lean on Amy. "I think I can balance it, at least for a while. It doesn't feel too bad if I don't *focus* on the memories. I can kind of pretend the human stuff is a film I watched."

Alastair peers into my eyes. "Are you—?"

"Don't ask me anything; don't make me look at the memories too hard, just let me get used to it." I exhale. It's like holding an overfull glass of water and running a race without spilling any of it. I've got to keep it all bottled up, but it wants to slosh over the sides.

Myrtle bobs down Amy's arm and nibbles my finger. Amy tuts and starts to push her away, but I stop her.

"Don't." I frown at the dove. "She's helping. She's so . . . weird. So is Elsie. They're helping me remember which memories are the real ones."

Dylan rubs his eyes. "My head . . .!" He sways. "I think it's happening to me too." He looks alarmed. "Did we do mock exams last week?"

Amy shakes her head. "*No!* Focus, Dylan. Look at Elsie." Then she exhales shakily, looking alarmed and almost as sick as I feel. "I'm not going to the all-girls school in Cambridge in September . . . am I?"

"No!" I say. "We all have to stay in Hockwold, at least till we're eighteen and our powers settle."

"P-powers?" she says.

"Look at Dolio!" I say.

We all look at Dolio, who is sitting in Hermes' palm looking as solid and real as it's possible for a tortoise to look. His perennially dusty shell is ridged, his neck scaly, and I'm sure he's smiling at me.

We drink him in.

"It's helping," I say. I look at Dylan. "What about you?"

"Yes." He looks relieved. Elsie grins up at him. "You're helping too, Elsie," he says. "What about you, Alastair?"

"Yeah." He looks pale and is gripping his locket again. "I'm feeling OK."

The sun is below the tops of the trees now and the sky is navy. The evening star glimmers on the horizon and the magpie shakes its black and white feathers on the church wall. At least it didn't follow us into Tartarus.

"We have to find the objects before we forget why we have to find the objects," I say.

Amy looks tearful. "But we've got no idea where to start, Hannah. No clues. Nothing!"

Alastair fingers his locket. "The staff is Hermes' object of power, right? Can he . . . well, can he sense it? Like, a magical connection."

We all look at Hermes. "Can you?" I say. "If you *can*, you could lead us right to it."

Hermes shakes his head. "I don't think so."

"At least try!" I fold my arms. "Close your eyes, picture it, and see if . . . well, if you want to head in any particular direction."

Hermes closes his eyes.

"Try turning in a circle," Dylan says after a moment.

Hermes extends his arms and turns around. Then he stops. He rotates back slightly, like a wobbling compass, and raises a finger, pointing. "It's that way!"

We march down the street in a strange procession. Hermes first, then me with Dolio, Dylan with Elsie, Amy with Myrtle and Alastair at the back. We pass Amy's house, where the tree – the site of my failed plan – still stands, bare of leaves and slightly smouldering. The smell of smoke lingers, and puddles soak into the grass where the fire department must have dampened the blaze. Amy hunches as we walk by, as if she expects her mum to burst through the front door, calling her name, but the house remains quiet.

We keep going. Hermes has one eye open, which is lucky because he tries to walk through Mr Hunter's hedge, and we are forced to take a route around.

"Hermes, can we go a bit faster?" Amy says. She's holding her head. "The human stuff . . . it's getting harder to hold back. I keep thinking I'm meant to be doing homework."

"Amy's right," I say. "I don't know how much longer we've got as ourselves."

Hermes nods and turns down Dylan's street, then into Dylan's front garden.

"What are you doing?" I catch his arm. "This isn't a short cut. It's Dylan's house. We'll have to go around again."

Hermes turns to me, and his eyes are no longer shining with humour. Nor is he smiling. "Hannah," he says. "We're not here for a short cut. My staff is right here."

He points at Dylan's garden shed.

CHAPTER TWENTY-TWO

THE SHED in Dylan's garden isn't really a shed. We just call it that. Mr Vine calls it his 'man-cave' and it's twice the width and height of an ordinary shed.

"I don't understand." I look at Dylan, but his expression is as confused as mine must be. I turn to Hermes. "Why would your staff be in Dylan's shed?"

"His pointing finger's off," Dylan says, with a frown. "Or he's playing one of his tricks. Hermes is famous for his tricks, remember Hannah? Or are those human memories messing with you?"

I shake my head. Hermes doesn't defend himself. He stands slightly apart from us, watching Dylan with narrowed eyes.

"Maybe we should take a look in the shed," Alastair says, suddenly sounding very serious.

Dylan stiffens. "Are you saying you don't trust me?"

"Of course we trust you!" I say. I look at Amy. "Don't we?"

There's a faint buzzing and the streetlights come on above us, creating pools of light on the pavement. The magpie flutters on to the shed roof, warbling bleakly. I narrow my eyes at it, wishing it would go away.

Dylan looks furious. Elsie moves to his side, turns to face us and her soot-coloured head growls, baring teeth like sabres. Amy gives a squeak of fear and Alastair hesitates, then he sprints for the garden path, curls bouncing as he runs.

"I'm opening that shed!" he shouts.

"Alastair, *no*!" I yell, as Elsie bounds after him, snarling, and Dylan gives chase.

Panicked, I turn to Hermes. "Grandad, you have to stop Elsie!"

"Oh, fine." He leaps skyward. His wings beat silently but raise dust clouds that make me cough. He moves almost faster than thought and reaches the shed before the boys, landing between Alastair and Elsie.

"*Elsie!*" He raises a hand. "Don't eat the kid!"

Elsie skids to a stop and Dylan throws an arm around her. Behind Hermes, Alastair, holding on to his pants with one hand, flings open the shed door and leaps inside. There is a beat of silence, then Alastair's voice floats into the garden.

"You guys." It reminds me of the moment we met this morning, him racing towards us. He called out 'you guys' then too – but this time his voice has a tone that scares me.

Glaring at Hermes, Dylan edges past, still holding on to Elsie, and goes inside.

I follow, bumping into Dylan's back when it becomes clear that he's halted in the entrance.

"Dylan?" He doesn't say anything, so I skirt around him. Then I stop too.

In the middle of Dylan's shed, surrounded by his dad's gardening tools and brewing kit, are the objects of power.

Aphrodite's apple gleams on the floorboards opposite Apollo's arrow, the gold skin reflecting a slice of the streetlight from the small window above. To the right of the apple, leaning against a shelf, Poseidon's trident stands upright, taller than Dylan. Further around, Hermes' staff lies on a crate of beer. Nearest us is Artemis's quiver, discarded on top of a box of seeds.

Against the back wall, Zeus's thunderbolt rests between Hephaestus's Hammer and the spear of Dionysus. Athena's shield is upside down under the window, like a sledge.

Alastair is standing beside the shield, staring at it.

Dylan is frozen, gaping like a ventriloquist's dummy.

Amy nudges me from behind and I move aside to let her in.

Hermes is right behind her. "Well, *that's* a relief," he says, gesturing towards the collection of objects. Hermes is reacting to their power, his hair standing on end, and the air around us all feels charged, like it does before a storm.

My own wings start to flutter, and I lift a few centimetres off the ground. It isn't a relief. Not at all. This is *Dylan's* shed.

"Why is everything *here*?" I sound like I'm about to cry and I barely even think about the fact that I've lost all my calm, which means I'm rising even higher. I don't need to worry though;

the shed has a roof.

Wordlessly, Alastair gestures; the missing marker stone is under the window, right in front of him.

We can restore the barrier, assuming that just putting the stone back in place will fix everything. But Zeus will still want to know who caused all this – and if it *was* something to do with Dylan, he'll be facing the wrath of the gods. Hermes was locked up for decades for a prank. What will they do to my best friend?

My head pounds and human memories seep into my thoughts, telling me that there are no gods and so, no problem. But at the same time, I'm floating above the floor. It makes no sense.

I wince and rub my temples.

"*Aphrodite's apple!*" Amy yells. Her expression cycles through relief, towards fury. "What *is* all this, Dylan?"

The gods are real, this is real. I grip Dolio so tightly that he nips my finger, and the human memories recede. Still floating in midair, I rotate towards Dylan. My eyes are now level with his, even though he's eight centimetres taller than I am. "Dylan, why are the objects in your shed?"

"I have no idea." He stares at me. "I didn't do this, Hannah. You have to believe me!"

I rise a little higher. Elsie glowers at me with all four eyes and growls again.

"Easy, Elsie," Hermes says.

"Everything was just here all this time?" Amy says.

Alastair looks sympathetically at Dylan. "I think it's time to confess, don't you, mate?"

"Confess?" Dylan stumbles back as if he's been struck.

"Yeah," Alastair says. He turns sad eyes on to me. "Why *were* you outside the barrier this morning? Whose idea was it to take a day off school?"

I gasp. "It was Dylan's idea . . ." I turn to him. "You said we should go to the Tree and practice our powers."

Dylan backs away. Elsie goes with him, loyally.

Amy catches my wrist, stopping me from hitting the roof, literally. She pulls me back down to her side.

Hermes slams an arm across the exit and Dylan is forced to change direction, moving until he hits the wall. Elsie plants her feet in front of him, heads looking in both directions, guarding him from us.

He looks genuinely upset. "What are you saying, Hannah?"

"Your spear was the only object not stolen," I whisper, my heart breaking. "The only one."

"*And* you hate your useless gift," Amy says. "Talking to dead grannies. Making strawberry laces. With all the objects of power, you'd be the strongest of our generation. Of *any* generation. No one would laugh at you ever again."

"Zack certainly wouldn't," I say. "Would he?"

Dylan whirls on me, and I see tears in his eyes. "You're meant to be my best friend, Hannah. I get that *she'd* believe this." He points at Amy. "And them." He points at Hermes and Alastair. "But you believe it too?" He turns towards the door, his shoulders sinking.

My heart hurts. I don't want to believe Dylan would do this, but the evidence is all here and, looking back over what's happened, it all adds up.

"Dylan," I whisper. "Did *you* burn the tree? You were last up the ladder. You could have set it on fire before you got on to the platform."

Dylan wheels around. "You think I'd risk hurting you?" He looks utterly betrayed.

Shouldn't *I* be the one who looks betrayed?

"I was with you *all day,* Hannah!" he says. "When could I have moved the marker stone?"

Hermes strides deeper into the shed, past Artemis's quiver. "*That's* mine, and I'm taking it." He points to his staff. "Try and stop me!"

"Why would I?" Dylan shouts. "*I didn't do this.*"

"Don't let him get away, Hannah!" Alastair yells.

Automatically, I reach to grab Dylan, and Elsie snarls, making me jump back, just as Hermes moves in reach of his staff.

As he steps into the centre of the shed, the five objects spread around the walls start to glow and lines of light appear between them.

"*Hermes!*" Amy shouts.

Dolio is a blur as he leaps from my hand but, before he can reach Hermes, he bounces back as if from a force field, and rebounds towards me. For a split second, I think I see tiny white wings on his legs, then they vanish. I catch Dolio like I'm catching a rugby ball and wrap both hands around his dusty shell, drawing him close to my chest. Dolio pulls his neck in, peering anxiously out.

"What in *Hades*?" Hermes shouts. He's completely frozen, one hand extended. His Hawaiian shirt hangs open and his wings flutter uselessly.

Then I see it. Five of the objects of power have not been tossed randomly in the shed; they're laid out very carefully. The lines connecting them create a shape.

"It's . . . a star?" I say, confused. I glance at Dylan, who looks as lost as I am.

"It's a trap," Amy says. "And Hermes just walked right into it!"

CHAPTER TWENTY-THREE

ALASTAIR IS stuck on the other side of the star, next to the marker stone and the remaining objects: the thunderbolt, the hammer, the spear and the shield. The star is glowing like a neon light.

"Alastair," I shout. "You have to get out of there, it's dangerous. Can you fit through that window behind you?"

Alastair turns. "I-I don't think so," he says. He turns back to me and a flush sneaks up his neck. "Thanks, though. I didn't know you cared."

Then he straightens.

It is as if he's been wearing a meek Alastair-suit all this time and now he's taking it off. His shoulders, which he has always held with a slight hunch, slide back. He rakes his hair out of his eyes and off his forehead . . . and he starts to laugh.

My eyes go to his T-shirt, where a star the same shape as the one imprisoning Hermes is slashed across his chest. Not a star: a *pentagram*.

"You're all so *stupid*." Alastair laughs. "You brought Hermes right here to me. I thought I'd have to spend *days* persuading you to free him. But I barely had to suggest it and off we went to Tartarus."

Amy covers her mouth. "*You* did this? Stole the objects and put them here? It was nothing to do with Dylan!"

Alastair snorts. "You think *Dylan* has the brains to pull off something like this?"

"Dylan, I'm so sorry." I reach for him, but he jerks away from me.

"Get over yourself, Dylan." Amy pulls her fingers through her hair so that it falls in gleaming curls down her back. Myrtle fluffs her wings and poops. "You can totally see how it looked bad."

"Now isn't the time for a *spat*, kids," Hermes calls. "I can't move and I'm not loving your mate's maniacal villain routine!"

I turn back to Alastair, my wings fluttering madly. "Why do all this? Why take all the objects? Why put them in Dylan's *shed*, of all places?"

Alastair sighs. "Because you'd never look here, would you? Not until I was ready. And if you *did* look here, well, all the evidence points to Dylan."

"But . . . you let us think . . ."

"Yeah. That was fun, for a minute," he says. "Seeing how strong your friendship *really* is. You're a smug twosome, you know?"

"Smug?" I stare at him. "Me and Dylan?"

"You think you have it hard because Zack and Zane are *mean* to you." He snorts. "Try having no friends *at all*. Try being the one picked last for *everything*. Try being one of the only kids in Hockwold who'll *never* get powers. Try being the one who . . ." he stops.

Amy frowns. "The one who what, Alastair?"

"The one who's nan dies, OK?" Alastair shouts. "Your grand-parents are immortal. Mine died."

"She did?" I glance at Amy, who looks stricken.

"Try being the one who gets called smelly because your mum is too depressed to wash your clothes. Try eating cereal every night for tea because she won't cook. Try . . ." He's crying now, great snivelling heaves. "Try being the one who gets called weird because you have to wear black because *she's* grieving and . . . and you are too . . . and she's thrown out all your other clothes!" He clutches his locket. "Try being *really* unhappy, Hannah." He glares at me. "Not, 'oh no, my parents don't pay me much attention'. Not, 'woe is me, I might grow up like a powerful god'. Not, '*waah*, Amy said something mean to me today'."

Amy flinches.

"Try *total misery*, Hannah. And no one . . . even . . . cares." He gasps into silence.

"I-I didn't know," I say, hoarsely.

"How could you?" Alastair snaps. "You never noticed me."

We stand awkwardly, unable to look at one another. Then Amy clears her throat. "I'm sorry, Alastair. We've been too wrapped up in our own stuff. All of us."

I nod. "I feel so bad about your nan. I didn't know."

"It was announced in assembly," Alastair says. "But it wasn't about you, was it? So you didn't pay any attention."

"Is that . . . hers?" I look at his fingers wrapped around the locket, and he drops them to his side and nods.

Inside the pentagram, Hermes has started to give off steam. "It's getting hot in here," he calls. "Now you've got all that off your chest, kid, can we talk about freeing the god in the five-pointed star?"

Alastair shakes himself and laughs. "Freeing you? No way. This is turning out just the way it's supposed to."

Amy frowns. "You said you wanted Hermes all along, which means you needed Hannah to take you to Tartarus. But . . . how did you know she wouldn't lose her memories along with everyone else?"

"That's the clever thing." Alastair smirks. "I've been manipulating Zack and Zane to pick on Dylan's rubbish power for *weeks*. All I had to do was wait for Dylan to snap and take off for the day. Hannah would go with him, *obviously*. Then I just had to set everything into motion. The marker stone, the objects of power – move them all into Dylan's shed, head towards the Tree to meet you, and *off we go*."

Amy blinks. "Then it was just dumb luck that I wasn't turned human, with everyone else."

Alastair sneers. "That's right. You should be just like Zack and Zane right now – clueless."

I am itching to grab him, but he's out of reach on the other side of one corner of the pentagram, and I don't want to know what happens if I put my arm through that glowing threshold. Dolio nips my finger comfortingly.

Amy whips round to look at me. "Your mum – this morning – she said your friend had been round."

I groan. "Of course . . . She never calls Dylan my 'friend'. He's always 'that awful boy'. It was *Alastair*!" I hang my head. "I should have known, Dylan."

He shrugs, but still looks hurt. I can fix this, but not now. Not when Hermes is trapped like a bug in a bottle.

I turn back to Alastair. "What do you need Hermes for?"

Alastair rubs his hands. "You mean the patron saint of burglars?" He waves like a commentator at a wrestling match. "The divine trickster? The prince of thieves?" He turns to Hermes with a wide grin on his face. "What do you think, Hermes? Has anyone ever carried off a robbery like this one? I've stolen the objects of power from the gods. Am I the greatest, or what?"

Hermes groans. "It's a coup, all right."

I glower at Hermes, and then at Alastair. "You want Hermes to tell you how good you are? Is that *it*? That's so *sad*!"

Alastair snatches up a beer bottle from a shelf and hurls it at my head. I duck and it shatters on the wall, spraying me with yeasty foam.

One of Elsie's heads barks, the other snarls and she leaps towards Alastair, right at the glowing pentagram. Dylan yells as she hits the line and there is a bang and an explosion of sparks. Amy screams as Elsie flies backwards, slams into the wall, then lies still.

Dylan kneels beside her.

"Is she . . ." I whisper.

He sits back. "She's alive." He leaps to his feet. "Alastair, you—"

"*That* was not my fault," Alastair yells. "You should have controlled your dog!" Then he calms down. "I need Hermes because I'm not done yet. This was just the warm-up. Now it's time for the main event!"

CHAPTER TWENTY-FOUR

"**THAT DOESN'T** sound good," Amy mutters, as Alastair turns to Hermes. "What's the main event?"

Alastair points to Athena's shield. "These objects focus the energies of each god. They have some power of their own, but they're trinkets compared to the true source of the gods' power and immortality." Alastair rubs his knuckles. "That's what I want – the source of the gods' power. I need a god to tell me where it is and how I can get hold of it. Hermes." He spread his hands. "Over to you."

I lunge forward, but Amy catches me.

"Careful." She points. The lines of the pentagram are singed into the wooden floorboards now, black lines that are starting to smoke.

"That's right," Alastair cackles. And I mean he *literally* cackles. "You can't touch this." He does a little dance, waving his hands in front of his face.

"Oh, *can't* we?" Amy snatches a rake from behind the door and uses the end to shove Artemis's quiver out of the pentagram. Or at least that's what she intended to do. The moment the rake touches the quiver, it bursts into flame. Amy drops it with a yelp, putting her hands under her armpits and stamping on the smouldering wood.

Alastair laughs. "Only an object of power can disrupt the pentagram and, oh, look, they're all over here, with me."

Dolio extends his neck from his shell. He glares at Alastair as if he can burn a hole in his forehead with the pressure of his lizard-like gaze.

"Don't you have enough power?" Dylan says, disbelievingly. "You've trapped a *god*, Alastair! With all these objects you can do practically anything. Why do you want more?"

"Dylan's right." I hold Dolio close. "The staff of Hermes gets you through any door – you can steal anything you want from the human world. With Aphrodite's apple, you can make anyone do anything. Why do you need the source of the gods' powers as well?"

Alastair glares. "That's what you'd do with the objects, is it?" He shakes his head and sneers again. "You're all so selfish. My ancestor stole fire from the gods, Hannah. He gave it to humans to help them. And you think I want to rob the very people he tried to save. Shame on you."

"Then you *don't* want to steal from the humans?" Dylan says, looking confused.

"No!" Alastair growls. "Aren't you *listening*? I'm going to take the source of the gods' power, then I'm going to give it *to the* humans. Prometheus offered them fire – I'm going to present them with so much more! No one will ever have to lose anyone they love ever again. Why should the gods be the only ones with power and immortality?"

We all stare at him.

"I'll be the most famous, the most adored, person in history. They remember the name Prometheus after all this time. Think how long they'll talk about Alastair Ignatius!"

I look for something to lean against and settle on a shelf behind me, groaning with old paint cans. "Alastair . . . I know I don't always pay attention in class, but I've got these human memories now, and, well . . . it's clear to me that humans don't do well with power. I mean, they've been at war with one another since the beginning of time. They've been destroying the climate, spreading diseases, making species extinct, blowing stuff up . . . do you *really* think giving them the power of the gods will end well?"

Amy rubs her eyes. "Hannah's right, Alastair. Humans aren't ready for our kind of power."

Alastair clenches his fists. "I don't care! No one in Hockwold likes me, but *they're* going to love me."

"Until they blow up the planet!" I shout.

"You don't know *anything*." Alastair yells. He whips around and faces Hermes. "Time to tell me – where's the source of the gods' power, and how do I take it?"

Hermes twists his eyes towards Alastair. "Hannah and her pals are right, kid. I can't tell you where the source of the gods' power is.

It's been hidden for millennia for a reason."

"I was afraid you'd say that," Alastair says, with frightening calm. Then he wraps his hand in an old cloth and closes his fist around the spear that is standing by his side, outside the glowing trap.

"Alastair, *no!*" Dylan yells. But Alastair raises Dionysus's spear, thrusts it through the lines of the pentagram and presses the end against Hermes' chest.

He holds it there, over his heart, and Hermes can do nothing but stand frozen as the spear lights up.

Dylan looks panicked. "Alastair, *stop!* You don't know what you're doing. Hermes is a *god*, and you're going to take away his inhibitions. There's no coming back from this!"

Alastair grins, his face lit up by the glow of the spear. "He should have told me where the power source is! Now he won't be able to stop himself from giving it up."

"*Hermes!*" I yell.

The spear goes dark, and Alastair pulls it back. "How are you feeling?" he smirks.

"Grandad?" I whisper.

Hermes giggles.

"The source of the gods' power," Alastair says. "Where is it?"

Hermes eyes are glazed, and he seeks mine out. "We're going to play so many tricks together, Hannah. So. Many. Tricks." His laugh is soulless, and I shiver.

Hermes idea of a trick was bad enough when he *had* limits. Remember the polar bear in Hera's pants? A trickster god with no restraints, no moral compass and no inhibitions could consider *anything* funny. Homicide. Genocide. An extinction-level event.

"Hecking Hades," Dylan whispers.

Alastair leans closer to the pentagram. "Tell me where the source of the gods' power is, and I'll let you out to play your tricks."

"Hermes," Amy shouts. "No!"

"I'll have my revenge against those who imprisoned me!" Hermes shouts. Then tears fill his eyes. "Oh, gods," he says. "The rock."

"Marvellous," Dylan says. "Now he's a *sad* drunk."

"Look what you've *done*, Alastair!" I yell.

Alastair clenches his fists. "Where is the source of the gods' power, Hermes? Tell me."

Hermes doesn't answer him. He fixes his eyes on mine. "The rock, Hannah," he whispers.

"He's right back in Tartarus!" I cry. "That's all he can think about – the rock he was chained to for over twenty years. He's not going to be able to tell you *anything*, you idiot!"

My wings flutter, my power coughs and my head hits the ceiling. Dylan and Amy grab me around the knees as I tilt towards the pentagram.

Amy's leap has forced Myrtle off her shoulder. The dove spreads her wings, gives her an annoyed peck and flies.

Amy screams as Myrtle heads towards the centre of the room, but as she passes above the nearest line of the pentagram, just above the tines of Poseidon's trident, nothing happens. She perches on the joist at the apex of the roof and looks down at me as if to ask what I think I'm doing.

I look down at Dylan. "Let go."

"No!" He tightens his grip.

"It's OK, I think." I look at Amy. "Let go, Amy."

Amy releases me, and I bob a little higher.

Myrtle ruffles her feathers and looks quizzical.

"Look at Myrtle, Dylan," I say. "The trap doesn't go past the top of the trident – I can get over it. I can get to Alastair."

"Don't you dare!" Alastair shouts. "You stay where you are, or—"

"Or what?" Dylan shouts. "Get him, Hannah!"

With Dolio in one hand, I stretch my arms out in front of me and throw myself forwards, trying to do a forward roll in midair.

For a moment, it feels as if Dolio is pulling me along. My feet come up, my back skims the ceiling and I fly past the shocked Myrtle. I land on my feet, right in front of Alastair.

But before I can do anything, except feel happy I'm alive, he shoves me hard with the hilt of the spear and I stagger backwards.

"Hannah!" Dylan yells. I catch hold of an old curtain rail and swing sideways, landing on the marker stone, which may be the size of an armchair but doesn't feel like one. The breath is knocked out of me.

"Did you think I wouldn't hit a girl?" Alastair crows. He steps towards me and Amy raises her hands, letting out a powerful shriek.

Nothing happens.

Alastair snorts and starts towards me again, raising the spear. Dolio struggles out of my hand, extending his neck, planting his forelimbs on the ground and hissing.

Before Alastair can strike me, the boards under our feet groan.

There's a blur of movement and Dolio appears on my chest. I grab him as the floor explodes. Splinters shower my face and I raise one arm to cover my eyes. When I lower it, there is a rose bush between me and Alastair. In seconds, it is waist high and bright red blooms are opening all over it.

"Ha!" Amy cries, gesturing wildly. "Suck it, Alastair!"

Dylan snatches a handful of strawberry laces from his pocket and throws them over the pentagram. They shower down on us. Alastair catches one and pops it in his mouth.

"Your power really is useless, isn't it, Dylan?" he says, chewing.

Dylan looks as if he's going to cry.

"And yours too, Amy." He walks around the rose bush. Then, in his free hand, he picks up the hammer of Hephaestus, the blacksmith.

"What are you going to do with that?" I shout. "Make me some horseshoes?"

Alastair shakes his head. "Actually, Hannah, I thought you might like some chains of your very own."

CHAPTER TWENTY-FIVE

ALASTAIR TOUCHES the marker with the hammer. Before I can escape, metal links snake from the sides of the cube-shaped rock and clamp around my wrists and ankles. I release Dolio, and he lands on my chest as the chains, cold and heavy, shorten and drag my wrists and ankles out to either side, leaving my back pressed against the stone.

"A couple of decades trapped here with a drunken Hermes should teach you a lesson, Hannah." Alastair hefts the hammer. "Unless you can get him to tell me where the source of the gods' power is. Then I'll let you both go."

Tears glitter on Amy's face, and I've never seen Dylan look so angry before.

"I'm sorry, Hannah," Amy sobs. "Alastair's right, we *are* useless. There's nothing we can do. We can't even go and bring someone to save you, because no one will believe us."

Alastair sniggers.

But I'm looking at Dylan. The way he's standing, with his fists closed and the expression of rage on his face, reminds me of the picture I saw in Amy's house. The one with Aphrodite, Dionysus and Hermes joined in battle.

I strain upwards. "Amy, listen! That picture in your house – the one your mum hates. She hates it because it shows Aphrodite as a warrior. *She* didn't just stand around growing roses, so you don't have to either. There must be more to your powers!"

Amy stares at me.

"Alastair has *completely* disrespected you, Amy," I call, as Alastair glares at me. "He planned for you to lose your memory along with everyone else. He stole Aphrodite's apple from under your nose. He thinks your powers are useless. He used you to help get Hermes for him! *What are you going to do about it?*"

Amy whirls around. She has finally stopped crying. Now she looks furious. With a shriek of rage, she thrusts a hand into the air, closes a fist and pulls it towards her.

Suddenly, she's holding a real-life, honest to goodness, *sword*.

It's half as big as she is.

"Hecking Hades, Amy!" Dylan yells, as she slashes at the pentagram. Sparks fly, but it doesn't affect the trap. Alastair relaxes, and Amy looks around for something else to hit.

"And what about you, Dylan?" I call. "Dionysus was in that picture too. He wasn't eating and drinking. He wasn't partying. He had a ghost beside him, and he was fighting, surrounded by snakes. *Snakes*, Dylan!"

Dylan pulls a handful of laces from his shirt pocket. "Snakes?"

He closes his eyes, and I can see him trying to find the calm Amy said we needed to control our powers. Then he tosses the laces over the pentagram. As the sweets reach their apex and Alastair starts to jeer, Dylan closes a fist . . . and suddenly the laces aren't laces any more.

Snakes rain down on Alastair, flicking their tails and baring their fangs. Dylan whoops.

I pull my feet up on to the stone as far as the chains will allow me. "Holy moly, Dylan!"

Alastair shrieks as the snakes hit the floor and start to wind their way towards him. He retreats towards the back of the shed.

"Stop it!" he cries. "Stop being so *mean*!"

"We were always meant to be friends, Amy!" I call. "Me, you and Dylan, working together, *fighting* together, to reach our full potential. That's what that picture was trying to tell us. That's why it never changed into something human. It was a message to the three of us from the gods."

Amy cries out and raises another fist. A whole *flock* of doves comes flying through the open shed door, until she stands in the centre of a whirlwind of feathers. She screams hoarsely and points, aiming them. They turn, as if with one mind, and zoom above the pentagram, heading for Alastair.

He ducks, still dancing to avoid the snakes.

I meet Hermes' eyes.

"Just like me," he says, and I realise he's staring at me sadly, chained to the stone.

"Yeah, I ended up just like you after all. Mum would be so proud."

Abruptly, Alastair's shouts turn from terrified to victorious. He drops the hammer and swings the spear in a circle, never touching the pentagram or the objects forming it. Whatever the spear touches, whether it is snake or bird, loses its focus.

Soon there are doves sitting all over the shed, on joists and beams, on the top of spades, looking even more confused than usual, and the snakes have abandoned their attack on Alastair and are winding their way out through the shattered floorboards.

"I can make more," Dylan shouts.

"And I can keep sending them away," Alastair replies. "You can't beat me! I'm too strong."

Dolio climbs off my chest and stands on the marker stone beside me. I turn my head to look at him. "Hey," I say. "Looks like I'm stuck here. You might as well leave. Dylan will look after you." I swear Dolio rolls his eyes. He shuffles to one side, drawing my attention and he taps with his claws.

"It's a rock, I know. I'm chained to it."

He looks at me and then at the stone, then at me, then at the stone.

Alastair comes to stand over me and I shiver. "Make Hermes tell me where the power source is," he says.

"How?" I blink up at him. "He doesn't even know what day it is."

Alastair rolls his eyes. "Maybe you both just need some motivation." He puts down the spear and picks up Zeus's thunderbolt, which still sits outside the pentagram. "I reckon this is gonna hurt him more than it hurts me, don't you?"

"Don't, Alastair! *Please!*" I turn a look of terror on the bolt. "I thought we'd become friends today."

Alastair looks sad for a moment. "Yeah. Weirdly, I had a good day with you guys. But it was only one day, Hannah. It wasn't enough to change the plan. I won't use this if you make him tell me what I want to know." He shakes the bolt. "If you don't, this is your fault, not mine."

I turn my face away, refusing to look, as the air grows more charged. My eyes fall on the spot Dolio is tapping. It's a worn part of the stone, more worn than the others. It has a pattern on it, a pattern that has always been there: ram's horns.

The ram is the sign of Zeus.

"Hecking Hades," I whisper, stealing the phrase from Dylan. "It's the *marker stone*. Is that what you're trying to tell me?" Dolio looks satisfied and pulls his head and feet back into his shell.

I whip my head around to look at Hermes who winks at me, just as Alastair releases a bolt of lightning. It crackles through the pentagram and detonates against his chest. I close my eyes as white light blazes and my head slams against rock.

Distantly, I hear Dylan and Amy screaming. Then everything goes quiet.

My human memories swirl in front of me in a series of pictures, like the photos in the hallway at home: Dylan and I at the local pool, sniggering as Amy tries to do butterfly stroke; the three of us in a rare truce, eating sweets under the Tree; Dylan teaching me to ride my bike; shopping for new wallpaper with Mum.

But these memories are only the life I might have had. They aren't real.

My real memories have emotions attached to them: confusion as I am told off for being too like Hermes, yet again; fear as I am presented to Zeus at the temple alongside Dylan and Amy; irritation at having to fill in the gods' family tree three times because I keep running out of space; jealousy when Mum brings Henry home; anger as Amy laughs when I practice my powers.

It doesn't matter, though, which memories are in front of me, human or inhuman. They all star Dylan, Amy, Mum, Dad and Henry. *They're* my family. I think of that family tree I had to draw and the line that connects Amy to her mum, to Aphrodite, to Zeus; the one that links Dylan to his dad, to Dionysus, to Zeus; the scrawl that I drew between me and Dad and Hermes and Zeus. Zeus connects us all. Our great-grandfather: King of the Gods.

It's OK that I remind Mum of Hermes. I come from him. And *he* comes from Zeus.

"I come from Zeus," I whisper.

Immediately, I feel clear-headed and weightless. I try to move my hands and feet, but I can't. They're still chained in place, but there's a part of me that isn't – part of me that connects to Zeus and the power of the gods – and that part is floating.

I turn my head. At first, the air around me is grey, as if I'm standing in soupy mist, but when I look harder, longer, I see that I am surrounded by glimmering specks and glowing seams of crystal. It's as if I'm looking hard at a piece of rock. Seeing more, seeing deeper. When I acknowledged that I was a part of Zeus, somehow my consciousness moved inside the stone. And the stone contains the source of the gods' power.

I open my fingers. The whole world is beneath my palms. The power of the gods crackles into me. But what should I do with it? My own words come back to me:

There must be more to your powers!

And then a memory of Dylan's voice rings in my ears.

Hermes is famous for his tricks, remember Hannah?

I am a part of Zeus. I come from Hermes.

I open my eyes.

Dylan and Amy are lying in a tangled heap on the ground, half-covered in junk. Hermes is still upright in the pentagram, but only because he can't move. He should be lying on the floor. There is a hole in his shirt and his chest hair is singed in a rough circle. Black veins run from the place Alastair hit him, all the way down to his jeans and up his neck. He looks dazed and his hair is smoking.

"Hermes?" Amy whispers. He doesn't answer.

Alastair raises the thunderbolt again.

"Wait!" I say. "I know where the source of power is!"

CHAPTER TWENTY-SIX

DYLAN LURCHES to his feet, shedding pots and gardening tools. "No, Hannah!"

"The source is right here," I say. "You had it all the time, Alastair. It must have been inside something else – Apollo's quiver, maybe. Your blast just knocked it loose."

Alastair follows my pointing finger and, using the power of the gods, I create an illusion.

"Rock, you see!" I say. "Hermes was trying to tell you."

Alastair is looking at a necklace. A long chain with a huge diamond pendant hanging from the centre. A big rock.

It is on the floor right beside him.

He picks it up and holds it in one hand, weighing the diamond. "*This* is the source of the gods' power?" he says.

"I think you have to put it on," I say.

Alastair peers at it closely. The sun shines through the small window and on to the rock. A prism of light bursts from the facets and catches the walls, making them glow with every colour of the rainbow. Alastair turns it; it is radiant.

"It makes sense," he says.

I look meaningfully at Dylan. He stares back at me.

Alastair slips the necklace around his neck. He pauses. "I don't feel anything," he says.

"Maybe you need to give it a minute," I say. I look at Dylan again and jerk my chin towards Alastair and the necklace, widening my eyes.

Dylan remains bemused.

"Oh, Aphrodite's apple, Dylan!" Amy snaps. She grabs his ear and whispers furiously. He whips around.

"What are you doing?" Alastair spreads his hands. "I have the power of the gods now. *You lose.* Everyone is going to love me!"

"It's a very pretty necklace," Dylan says. Then he tilts his head. "Or . . . is it?"

I let the illusion drop.

The necklace turns back into a length of garden hose just as Dylan raises his fist.

Suddenly, Alastair has a snake around his neck. It hisses.

Alastair freezes.

"Free Hannah and Hermes and I'll make it let you go," Dylan says.

Alastair clenches his fists, and then sags. "Fine. Y-you win," he says, with angry tears shining in his eyes.

Moving with extreme care, he uses the tip of Zeus's thunderbolt to roll the apple out of the pentagram.

The lines glow for another heartbeat then vanish. Hermes hits the floor, his palms slapping on the splintered boards.

"Now release Hannah!" Amy says, raising her sword.

Shaking, Alastair picks up the hammer, presses it against the stone and my chains melt away. I pick up Dolio, drop him inside my shirt and climb off the rock. Then I help Amy lift Hermes. He stumbles to his feet, swaying, and we gather by the fallen Elsie.

"I've done what you said," Alastair rasps. "Now get it off me!"

Myrtle flutters from the roof and lands on Amy's shoulder. She relieves herself down Amy's back. I don't even smile.

"Dylan, *please!*" Alastair whispers.

Dylan glances at me and I nod. He gestures and the snake turns back into a hose. Alastair pulls it away from his throat and throws it as hard as he can.

Then he shoves past us, and races into the night. I hear the sound of a magpie warbling, and then there is quiet.

Dylan starts to go after him, but I catch his arm. "What about Grandad?" I say. "Can you use the spear to sober him up?"

Hermes dangles between us, giggling and muttering. "Tricks! Tricks!"

"It's OK, Grandad," I say, knowing it isn't. "We'll get you fixed up."

"I don't think I can," Dylan says, miserably. "With a dose as strong as the one Hermes got, the damage is permanent."

"Won't you even try?" I ask.

Reluctantly, Dylan covers his hand with his T-shirt and picks up the spear. "I don't even know how to use this," he says. "I might make him worse."

"Wait." I point to the boundary stone. "What if you're touching that?"

"The old marker?" Amy says, with a frown.

I nod. "It's the source of the gods' power."

"Are you *serious*?" she gapes. Then she looks at Hermes. "Is that why Hermes kept saying '*rock*'? Was he trying to answer Alastair the whole time?"

"I think he was trying to tell me what to do. Either way, we can't leave him like this." I shift my weight to keep Hermes from falling.

"All right then, I'll try." Dylan steps over Poseidon's trident and makes his way to the stone. Then he puts one hand on it. "Nothing's happening."

"I think the stone has to recognise your connection to the power of the gods," I say. "Tell it you come from Zeus."

"I come from Zeus," Dylan says, awkwardly.

"You have to mean it, Dylan," Amy says.

"I come from Z—"

His head is thrown back, and his eyes start to shine as if someone has switched a powerful torch on inside his head.

"Wow!" Amy staggers. "Dylan, are you OK?"

Instead of answering, he raises the spear.

"You'd better get out of the way," he says, his voice resonating oddly from the wooden walls.

We help Hermes sit up, then step away. Amy drives her sword into the air, opens her fist, and it vanishes as if she's sheathed it.

I take her hand. She squeezes it and her dove coos. Dolio watches, doing nothing. Somehow, I think that if this was dangerous, he'd let me know. Maybe. Probably.

"Do it, Dylan," I shout.

Dylan pushes the spear towards Hermes. He touches his chest with the tip and again a purple glow fills the shed. Then Dylan lets go of the stone and sags to his knees.

Hermes groans and tilts sideways. I jump to catch him. Dolio hops out of my hand and sits on his knee, tapping him with his claws.

Finally, Hermes opens his eyes. "Dolio?" He clears his throat. "That tortoise – been keeping me sane for centuries." He looks at me. "Hannah. Well done, kid. Rock, right?"

"Rock." I exhale shakily. "You scared the poop out of us!"

His smile looks a little tired. "I'm a *god*, Hannah, what else did you expect?" He hands Dolio to me, bounds to his feet and rubs his hands. "Right, where is that little monster?"

"He ran off," I say. I avoid Hermes' eyes and rub my wrists. "And . . . that's probably a good thing."

"A *good* thing?" Dylan gets to his feet and stares. "Are you kidding?"

I shake my head. "I'm serious. Alastair nicked all the gods' stuff and tried to give the source of their power to the humans. Imagine what Zeus will do to him!"

"Don't forget he nearly killed us," Amy says. "He must have set fire to my tree the moment we were out of sight."

"His nan died," I remind them, miserably. 'I can't imagine how

I'd feel if I lost my family. I don't think we can blame him for what he did. Not completely."

Hermes groans. "The kid's eleven. He'll be a thousand before the fam finishes punishing him. If they ever do."

We look at one another.

"Well, what do we do then?" Dylan says.

Hermes sighs. "*I'll* take the blame."

Amy stamps her foot. "*No way!* They'll put you back in Tartarus. Naked. Covered in honey and wasps."

"Don't worry, kiddo." He winks. "I've got a few tricks up my sleeve." He strides to the marker stone. "You kids return the objects and, once I'm feeling up to it, I'll put this back where it's meant to be." He looks absolutely wrung out.

"Are you sure?" I say. "We could—"

Dylan looks at me. "It's a pretty big rock, Hannah. I think Hermes is going to have to be the one who moves it."

Something tickles the back of my mind. Something important. I roll my thoughts around like I'm trying to get a pip out of my teeth. I almost have it. Something about the marker stone . . .

Elsie raises her head and yips pitifully.

"Elsie!" Dylan sounds delighted and, in the joy of stroking his dog, I forget all about it.

And this, you could say, turns out to be my biggest mistake.

Yes – even bigger than the terrible plan that lost us the spear.

CHAPTER TWENTY-SEVEN

ONCE ELSIE is on her feet and panting happily with both heads, we look at the objects scattered around the shed: Zeus's thunderbolt, Aphrodite's apple, Artemis's quiver, Apollo's arrow, The Hammer of Hephaestus, Poseidon's trident and Athena's shield. The objects held in trust by the families of the gods.

Hermes sits on the marker stone, patting his staff as if it's an overexerted toddler. Dylan grips the spear like he's never going to let it go.

The air feels charged; it buzzes with an undercurrent of power. I shiver. "We need to separate everything, right now – it feels like a storm in here."

Amy picks up Aphrodite's apple, checks the golden skin all over for bruises, polishes it with her sleeve and slips it into her pocket. She noticeably relaxes, then she frowns at the other objects.

"Shouldn't there be twelve?"

I shake my head. "Alastair *never* could have got the helm of Hades from the underworld, and Hera took her ring with her."

Dylan mutters under his breath and I realise he's ticking off his fingers. "*Number one, at the top, is Zeus the king; Hera's the goddess who wears his ring; Poseidon, his brother is God of the Sea; From which came the beautiful Aphrodite. Athena, most wise, emerged from his head; Another brother, Hades rules the world of the dead; Dionysus is god for parties with bunting; But Artemis is best if you want to go hunting; Her twin, bright Apollo, is God of the Sun; But if you want a fight, Ares is the one . . .*" He stops before he gets to Hermes. "Ares' sword!" he says. "Didn't he take it with him to Afghanistan?"

I laugh. "You needed that dumb preschool rhyme to work out what was missing?"

Dylan flushes and I pick up the thunderbolt. It is surprisingly light. "We should return these, before everyone gets their memories back." I look at Hermes.

He nods. "You don't want to be caught by the fam with your hands on their stuff." He rubs his singed chest and glances at his watch. "I'll give you exactly one hour – I'll replace the stone at nine o'clock. Will that be enough time?"

I slide the thunderbolt carefully into a belt loop and pick up Athena's shield. "We'll work together." Dolio looks at me expectantly and I bend down and open my bag. He gives Hermes what I consider to be a meaningful look, then crawls inside.

"Oh, all right." Amy exhales. She doesn't look particularly happy, but she takes Apollo's arrow and drops it into Artemis's quiver.

Dylan hefts the hammer with his free hand.

"That leaves Poseidon's trident," I say. "Can anyone manage that?"

Amy nods, slips the quiver over her shoulder, and picks up the trident. It's taller than she is. Myrtle looks at the three sharp prongs as if considering whether to roost on one of them.

"Trident first?" I say, and Amy nods.

Poseidon's son, Mr Seaver, lives with his husband down a lane with wide-reaching views of the Fens. Not that we can see them in the dark, although I can make out the glimmer of stars on the water.

We walk together, the thunderbolt knocking against my thigh, the *tap, tap* of the trident on the pavement. The air still feels filled with static, and the hairs on my arms prickle uncomfortably. I rub my free hand over the back of my neck and hear the *'kah-kah . . . kah-kah-kah'* of the magpie from a nearby hedge.

"Shouldn't that thing be roosting by now?" Amy snaps, and Dylan kicks a rock towards it. It launches into the sky, its white stomach flashing, its screech fading as it climbs.

"My human memories are getting stronger by the minute,' Amy mutters. "I keep thinking we have a grammar test tomorrow. *And* it's getting cold."

The reflected pinpoints of light start to wink out in the Fens, and I look up. Clouds are boiling overhead, blotting out the stars.

"Hecking Hades," Dylan says, staring at the sky. "That's a

big storm. Does it feel to you guys as if . . . as if something bad is coming?"

"Could it be something to do with the objects?" I wonder, as the darkness gathers and the shadows close in.

"How can it be?" Amy says, as Dylan strides faster towards the lights on the Seavers' driveway.

"We just have to get everything back into place," I say. "As fast as we can."

We run to catch up.

In the real Hockwold, the Seavers' vaguely conch-shaped house is surrounded by dozens of fountains and pools, so many that if you squint it really does look as if it is nestled among waves. In this new, human Hockwold, they own a wood-fronted eco-lodge, with an algae-filled pond out front and a trickling fountain beside the front steps. There are solar-powered lights on the path, which is how I know the house is painted blue.

We come to a stop in front of the fountain, Zeus's thunderbolt rattling against my thigh. A droplet of rain hisses against it as Amy gestures with the trident. "Where do we leave this?"

Dylan looks around, as if worried someone has followed us. "We should get it inside at least," Dylan says. "In case Alastair is still around."

"How?" Amy says. "Ring the doorbell and hand it back?"

Dylan looks horrified. "And when their memories are restored, who will they come to, demanding answers? *Us! I* don't want to end up chained to a rock."

I bite my lip. Dolio pokes his head from my bag but is otherwise unhelpful and Myrtle coos from on top of the trident. Also useless. Elsie drools on my shoe.

A light goes on inside the house and, moments later, the distant laughter of a television show.

"I hate to say this," I say, shoulders sagging. "But . . . there is another option." I pull Alastair's lockpicks from my pocket.

Dylan drops the hammer and takes my arm. "You've still got those? Your mum would go mad."

"I know." I swallow. "But I can do this." I start to climb the steps to the front door.

Amy stops me with a shake of her head. "What if we unlock the door and they're right there, going '*what do you kids think you're doing?*'"

"They're watching TV," I say. "We just need to open the door, put the Trident in the hallway, shut the door again and run."

Another raindrop hits my forehead.

"Go on then," Amy says, but her expression is miserable. A bead of rain on her cheek looks like a tear. In fact, she hasn't seemed happy since we left Hermes with the marker stone. But I can't dwell on that now.

I bend over in front of the lock and unroll the cloth, trying not to think about Alastair doing the same thing before he coached me in Tartarus. I have an odd moment of missing him, which I put down to my human memories telling me none of this is real, then I select a much smaller pick and slip it into the lock.

More rain falls on my bent back and steams from Zeus's thunderbolt. I frown in concentration, feeling for the moment the pick reaches the right angle and lifts the tumbler. There's a faint click, and I hold it still as I insert the next.

"Come *on*, Hannah," Dylan whispers. I ignore him.

Thunder rumbles overhead. I wiggle the shafts and, suddenly, the lock is open.

"Quick," I gesture to Amy, and she hands me the trident. I shift Athena's shield on to my forearm and step into the house.

CHAPTER TWENTY-EIGHT

THE SEAVERS' hallway is also blue and papered with hanging seascapes. Moving like a ghost, I lean the trident against the nearest wall, careful not to let it knock against any of the pictures.

I listen, but the television is still on and it doesn't seem that the Seavers have noticed their open front door.

I am about to turn and head back out of the house, when something catches my ear. The sound coming from the television changes from canned laughter to '*Breaking News*'.

My curiosity overcomes my fear and I start to edge my way deeper into the house. What *Breaking News*?

"What are you doing?" Dylan whisper-shouts from the front steps. "Come back!"

The living room is at the front of the house; the Seavers are sat together on the sofa, their eyes pinned to the screen. I hold my hand in front of my mouth, in case they can hear me breathing, and stand by the doorway, watching. The newsreader is clutching her papers with white knuckles and there are lines of tension around her eyes. She seems frightened.

'A chain of natural disasters has occurred around the world: earthquakes in America, tsunamis in the Pacific, wildfires in Australia and volcanic eruptions in Europe. Here in the UK, the met office has delivered flood warnings for the South-East and South-West, while the North-East and Scotland are warned to brace themselves for blizzards. While these astonishing unseasonal weather fronts appear to have come from nowhere, Professor Jim Hall of Oxford University says . . .'

The Seavers continue to stare at the screen, not hearing my small gasp.

Could this be *our* fault? Something to do with the gods, or their objects of power? I look at the shield still held in front of me. How could this be causing a fire in Australia, or even a blizzard in Scotland?

Or, like Dylan said, is something else coming?

But . . . I messed with the *source* of the gods' power. When I was inside it, I felt that connection to the whole world. Could *I* have caused this?

This time my sound of distress snags the attention of the Seavers, and I fling myself flat behind the sofa, thankful for their thick carpet, which cushions my landing. The bag containing Dolio bumps my shoulders and I hold Athena's shield out in front of me. I smell burning and look down. The carpet is smouldering where it touches the thunderbolt. I pat at it frantically.

"What was that?" The son of Poseidon stands up. His dark head rises over the top of the sofa.

You can't see me, I think. *There's nobody here.*

He walks out from the front of the sofa and around it, and I know that I am caught. I hold my breath.

I'm nobody. You can't see me. I'm not here.

"What is it?" his husband asks. "What did you hear?"

"I don't know." Mr Seaver stands right above me, frowning at the space over my head. "There's no one here." He sniffs and I know he can smell singed carpet. But he still doesn't look at me.

My eyes widen. Is invisibility in my blood? A power of Hermes? If so, why hasn't Dad ever mentioned it?

"You're just jumpy, Caspian," his husband says. "Sit back down. If there are going to be floods, we need to make plans."

"You're right." Mr Seaver scratches his chin and shifts his gaze to the floor just beyond me. My chest is burning with the need to breathe, but I don't dare make a sound.

I'm not here, I think. *Not here.*

My heart is pounding. It hammers in my ears so loudly I can barely think. Finally, Mr Seaver returns to his place on the sofa.

Then, human thoughts wash over me like a wave. *I can't be invisible. I don't have powers. I'm only a normal girl.*

And I know that if they turn around now, they'll see me.

I dare to take a small breath, forcing myself not to gasp as if I've just swum underwater for half a mile, then I commando crawl out of the living room, The thunderbolt makes every movement awkward. Once in the hallway, I stand and race for the front door, bag bumping against my spine, my little ankle wings fluttering with anxiety.

Ankle wings – I'm *not* human! I'm *not*.

Ignoring Dylan's irritated "*What are you doing, Hannah?*", I pull the door closed, then I take the steps two at a time. It is really raining now, and Amy looks half-drowned. A bedraggled Myrtle huddles on her shoulder, using her hair as shelter.

"There's something wrong with the world," I gasp. "It was on the TV. A whole bunch of natural disasters. It has to be our fault, but I just don't get it."

"How can it be *our* fault?" Amy has to raise her voice to be heard over the rain.

"It can't be a coincidence, can it?" I lift Athena's shield over us like an umbrella and she sighs in relief. "Something goes wrong with the gods, and something goes wrong with the world."

"That would make it *Alastair's* fault then," Amy snaps, and she starts stalking towards the road. "Come on, let's get this over with."

Dylan pushes his wet hair out of his eyes and ducks under Athena's shield. Rain drums on the curved metal and streams down the sides. Elsie presses herself against his leg, trying to stay in the dry.

"Are you OK?" he asks. "You seem . . ."

"It's my memories." I hold the shield tighter. "I'm barely holding on to them."

He nods. "Same here, I hate it. But we're almost done, right?" He looks at the rain. "There's really something wrong with the world?"

I nod. "Floods, blizzards, fires, earthquakes, volcanoes . . ."

"Oh." He swallows. "Do you think it'll all go back to normal when we've returned the objects and the stone?"

"I hope so." I look at Amy's retreating back, her hair beads glimmering in the darkness, and catch a glimpse of the magpie's white feathers flashing overhead. I curl a lip at it. "I really hope so."

The nearest house to the Seavers is that of the Hephaestus, or Smith, family. Hephaestus and his dad weren't historically best buds, if you know what I mean. And being Aphrodite's ex means he's not exactly welcome in town, so he built a place on the outskirts. Not as far out as Poseidon's lot (who prefer fish to people), and generally closer to the centre of things than the honorary Hockwoldians, like Alastair's family, but still far enough from the green so that he doesn't risk bumping into the other gods when he's out for a walk.

And yes, this means we have to get the hammer past the *actual* Hephaestus *and* his six-foot-tall daughter, who has a booming voice and wears rings like weapons on every knuckle. She also has twin toddlers, who don't worry me. They, at least, should be in bed by now.

Dylan crouches behind the garden wall, clutching the hammer to his chest, one hand on Elsie's back. "You mean you can sneak in, without being seen? You're sure?"

"The Seavers looked right at me," I say. "It must be something to do with the way we learnt how to fight back there. You can make snakes now, Amy has a whopping great sword and I'm . . . stealthy. Tricksy."

"I have a sword?" Amy says. Then she frowns. "That's right, I do."

"Hold on, Amy," Dylan says. "It's your human memories, we'll be rid of them soon." He touches my shoulder. "What about Hephaestus, Hannah? He's a god. Can you sneak past *him*?"

"I have no idea." I hand Dylan the shield and take the hammer. "But I'm going to have to take the risk."

It turns out that it isn't Hephaestus I have to worry about.

CHAPTER
TWENTY-NINE

I STAND IN the porch of the Smith house, with one toddler hanging off each leg.

"Get *off*!" I hiss. They're feral, bright eyes staring up at me from beneath matching thatches of auburn hair, sticky fingers grappling my trousers and filthy animal-print onesies adding to the impression that they'd be better locked in a cage somewhere. I'd certainly be happier if they were.

I'd barely had a chance to sneak through the front door and look for somewhere to leave the hammer when they barrelled out of nowhere and clamped themselves to me. I didn't have time to try my invisibility trick.

One of them giggles and reaches for the thunderbolt, while the other roars and bites my shin. I yelp and bat the reaching hand away. Thankfully, there is no sign of their mum. Loud snoring emanates from a room just ahead of me, so I assume the twins have defeated every adult in the house.

What do I do? I can hardly creep back out with these two attached.

"Dylan," I call through clenched teeth. "*Help!*"

Dylan appears silhouetted against the rain. "Hannah, what . . . oh!"

"Get them *off* me!"

"How?" Dylan drops to his knees. "Hi little . . . kiddies . . . why don't you leave Hannah alone?"

One of them shakes his head so hard his eyeballs must be in danger of rolling out of their sockets. The other, the roaring one, sinks his teeth deeper into me.

I have to bite my own wrist to muffle my scream. "*Dylan!*"

He looks frantically around as if a solution might present itself. Then his hand claps his shirt pocket and his eyes narrow. "How about some sweets?" he says.

The toddlers look interested.

"Let Hannah go, and I'll give you more strawberry laces than you can eat."

He pulls handful after handful out of his pocket and the twins gape, like he's Father Christmas. Then Dylan tosses the laces down the hallway. I am reminded of the moment Alastair threw Dolio for Elsie, then the twins vanish from my legs as if they've teleported. I run for the door, coming face-to-face with Amy.

"You can't leave it *there!*" She points. I've dumped the hammer against the wall by the coat rack. "You can't leave the hammer of Hephaestus in reach of *toddlers!*"

"For the love of Hera!" I turn back, grab the hammer, reach up and balance it on top of the hooks. "Better?"

Amy nods.

"Can we run now?"

We run.

"How much longer before Hermes puts the stone back?" I shout, scuttling along under the shield that Dylan is now holding over us. Dylan looks at his watch. "Twenty minutes."

"We still have the shield, the quiver, the arrow and the thunderbolt," I gasp, holding my side. "And my head is hurting. We don't have enough time. We're going to have to split up."

Amy sighs so loudly I hear her over the pounding rain. "I suppose you want me to return the thunderbolt to Zack's house?"

I pull it out of my belt loop and hand it to her. "Thanks for offering."

We separate when we reach the village green. Dylan takes the quiver and arrow, I take the shield, Amy already has the thunderbolt.

"All right, you guys," I say, holding the shield above our heads. "Meet back here when we're done?"

"Actually, I have to take the apple home and I want to check on Mum," Amy says. "And don't you want to return the spear and make sure *your* parents are OK?" She says to Dylan.

"I suppose." Dylan looks at me. "We don't *have* to meet back up. We'll know everything's OK and Hermes has returned the stone when everyone goes back to normal, and we should probably be home when that happens so no one gets suspicious." He has to raise his voice over the drumming of the rain on the shield above us.

Amy shuffles her feet, awkwardly. "So, I'll just . . . see you at school tomorrow then?"

"Yeah." Dylan looks equally awkward. "See you."

She strides towards Hockwald Hall, disappearing into the darkness and the rain.

Dylan straightens. "Right, you take the shield to the Wisdom's house while I go to the Hunter's."

"How will you get in?"

Dylan shrugs. "You're not the only one with skills, Hannah." I make a face at him, and he pauses. "I'll shove it through the cat flap."

"Good idea." I clear my throat. "Look, I really am sorry about the whole . . . thing in the shed."

Dylan looks at his feet. "Whatever."

"No, I should never have doubted you. I should have known it was Alastair. I could have stopped him sooner if . . ."

"It's fine." Dylan's smile is forced. "Everything turned out OK."

"And . . . *we're* OK?" I ask.

He nods.

"You're still my best friend?" I say in a voice I can barely hear over the rain. "I'll never doubt you again. I promise."

Dylan rubs his forehead. "Even in my weird human memories, you're my best friend, Hannah. Not much about them is right, but that is."

"Same here," I say, my heart feeling lighter.

He looks at his watch. "We'd better get going. I'll see you tomorrow." Suddenly, he grins. "It'll be strange, no one knowing what we've done."

"It better stay that way!" I narrow my eyes. "Mum would ground me for life if she knew what I'd been up to today!"

Dylan ducks out from under the shelter of the shield. Immediately, the rain flattens his hair. He salutes me with the spear and then he too is gone.

The Wisdom's house is just down the road from mine. I sneak in through the back door this time and leave the shield on the kitchen counter, relieved to be out of the wet before I hustle back out. Without the shield, I have nothing to shelter me from the storm. I look up and rain fills my eyes and drags my hair down my back.

I wonder if Amy has managed to get the bolt back on to its hooks, without being trapped with Zack. I wonder how close Hermes is to returning the stone. I rub my head again, as new thoughts flood me, telling me there is no bolt, no Hermes, no stone.

Then I turn and run home, splashing through puddles all the way.

CHAPTER
THIRTY

MUM, **DAD** and Henry are in the kitchen. Mum looks up when I creep in.

"You're soaking, Hannah! Don't sit on the furniture, get a towel."

"Yes, Mum."

I glance at the kitchen clock on my way to the bathroom – just two minutes left, and everything will go back to normal. I wonder how it'll happen: will it all just *snap* back into place? Like, a blink and everything is changed? Or will reality appear like a wave, rinsing humanity away piece-by-piece?

I can't wait to have my false human memories washed out of my mind.

Then I frown. What a strange thing to think. I *am* human.

I pick up a towel and rub my hair. Dolio pokes his head out of the bag and I give him a pat. "Good boy." I wander back into the kitchen still holding the towel, my socks squishing damply in my shoes.

A thought occurs to me: I want to see Mum and Dad turn back into themselves. I miss them.

Then I shake my head. Turn back into *themselves*? I must be going mad. Who else would they be?

I feel sick, as if something precious is streaming out of my head but I don't know what it is I'm losing.

The clock is ticking closer to the hour. The rain beats on the window, and I jump as something hits the glass.

Dad leaps to his feet. "What on earth is that?"

I place my hands on the pane and squint into the darkness. "I don't—"

And then the something hits the window again. It's a dove, feathers spiky from the rain, dishevelled and bloody.

Why would a dove be . . .?

And then I remember her. "Myrtle!" I reach for the latch.

"Hannah!" Mum snaps. "Don't you dare open that window. Honestly. What's got into you?"

"Fine!" I race from the kitchen, open the front door and plunge into the storm. "Myrtle?" I shout, holding out an arm. Mum is shouting behind me.

Moments later, the dove wobbles out of the sky and lands on my hand, gripping with claws like pins.

I return to the hallway. Myrtle huddles into her wings, looking up at me with beseeching eyes. A trickle of blood runs down my wrist.

"Hannah!" Mum is standing by the kitchen door, holding Henry. "What are you *doing*?"

"It's Amy's bird," I say. At least I think it is. My heart thumps. "I think Amy's in trouble."

"Don't be ridiculous, Hannah. Why would Amy be in trouble?" She looks behind her. "Right, Herman?"

"That's right." Dad appears, looking serious. "We're having a family meeting, Hannah. There's a flood warning, and we were talking about going to stay with your aunt in Sheffield, where it's higher ground."

There was something important about the time, something I had to remember.

"What time is it? Dad, get out of the way!" I ignore Mum's sound of shock and push past him into the kitchen. The clock has ticked past the hour.

Terror grips me, but I don't know why. What was meant to happen on the hour? Why was it so important?

Myrtle nips the web of skin between my thumb and forefinger, and I yelp.

"The stone!"

Hermes should have returned the stone by now, but our kitchen table remains stubbornly Ikea and there is no sign of the family hearth.

Worse, my human thoughts are still there, like an abscess, leaking all over my brain and drowning me in mundanity.

I blink a few times, but nothing changes.

"Hannah, you're being very rude!" Mum stands behind me.

"Why are you staring at the clock?"

I turn to her. "Mum . . . do you feel any different?"

"Different, Hannah?" She frowns at me. Henry reaches out a hand and I take it, trying to smile at him.

"I mean, if I asked you about . . . about Grandad's staff, the one from the living room, what would you say?"

"That old thing? Hannah, are you feeling ill? Do you need to go to bed?"

I shake my head and drop Henry's hand. Myrtle coos worriedly.

"Something's gone wrong, Mum." Tears prick my eyes.

Dad gives me one of his looks and I swallow. "Listen, you guys, I'm . . . going to take Myrtle back to Amy's house. She must have . . . escaped her cage."

Mum looks at Dad. "What do you think, Herman? It's not weather to be out in."

"Put a coat on," Dad says.

I race back into the street, zipping my coat as I go. There's no point going to Amy's house. The last place she was headed was Hockwold Hall and, if I go via the green, I'll be able to see what Hermes is up to with the stone. Maybe he just needs a hand. It is really heavy.

I pause. It is really, *really* heavy.

"Hannah, you *idiot*!" Ducking to keep the rain out of my eyes, I pull my hood up over my head, pop Myrtle inside to keep her dry, adjust Dolio's bag and sprint towards the green.

That's what my brain was trying to tell me. There is no way that Alastair moved that stone by himself!

He wasn't working alone.

The dark and the rain make it difficult to see and so, when I reach the green, I'm relieved to find the streetlamps illuminating the central cross and the space where the marker stone ought to be. There is no sign, however, of the stone or of Hermes.

"Grandad?" I yell, and head on to the grass, which is rapidly turning into mud as sticky as if Dylan has used the spear on it. "Amy?" A rising wind snatches my call and delivers it to the sky unheard. Myrtle's claws dig into my shoulder, and she coos nervously.

My shoes slide on the boggy ground and my hair falls out of the hood and into my eyes in wet strands. I push them away and turn towards Hockwold Hall. That's when I see them, standing at the edge of the green, orange light highlighting their outlines.

"Grandad!" I jog towards him, only remaining upright because my wings keep fluttering and lifting me out of the worst puddles. Hermes doesn't turn.

He is crouching next to Amy, Zeus's thunderbolt in one hand and his staff tucked into his belt. The marker stone is lying out of place on the pavement, directly in the shaft of light cast by a streetlight. Amy stands next to him, holding Aphrodite's apple out in front of her. It glows.

Her hair curls down her back in wet snakes, beads snatching the light. Her mouth is a flat, determined line, and on her shoulder, instead of Myrtle, sits the magpie.

One for sorrow.

On my shoulder, Myrtle grumbles, and her claws dig deeper into my skin.

"Amy!" My feet slide in the mud as I hurry towards her. "What's going on? Why did Myrtle come to find me? And what are you doing with that magpie?"

Dolio's head pops out of my bag. He stares at the magpie and suddenly my bag is one tortoise lighter. I locate him crouching on the grass at my feet. He moves one foot back and then the other. It looks as if he's about to run a race. As I watch, miniature wings appear on the backs of his legs, there is a tiny thunderclap, and Dolio vanishes.

OK then.

My human memories try to tell me I can't have seen that. Then they give up and recede a little more. I take a breath to steady myself.

"Amy?" I stare between Amy and Hermes. She doesn't even acknowledge my arrival. The magpie presses itself closer to her cheek. The apple glows more brightly. "Are you in trouble?"

"Do it, Hermes," Amy says. "Destroy the stone!"

CHAPTER THIRTY-ONE

HERMES RAISES his arm and points the thunderbolt at the stone. Without thinking, I hurl myself across the grass and smash into his arm. Myrtle takes off, wings whistling, and I slam Hermes to the ground, like a pro-rugby player.

He lands, rolls and bounces back up, still holding a fistful of lightning. His eyes are glazed.

"Grandad, what are you—"

The bolt hits the marker stone like a bomb going off. I scream and roll, with my hands over my ears. "*Grandad!*"

"Must destroy the stone," he mutters. At least I think that's what he says. My ears are ringing. The smoke clears, leaving the stone looking singed. One corner seems to have been knocked off, but it is otherwise unharmed.

Thank Hera.

"Again!" Amy shouts, and Hermes raises the bolt.

It'll be no good deflecting Hermes' aim every time – it's Amy I have to stop. Is her human self *evil*? Is that why a magpie has replaced Myrtle?

I scramble to my feet and throw myself at her, grappling for the apple. It is slippery with rain and impossible to grip, so I try to slap it out of her fist. Finally, Amy turns her attention towards me.

"Stop it, Hannah," she yells. "This is the right thing to do!"

I try for the apple again, wings fluttering to propel me forwards. "How is this the right thing to do?" I scream. "That's the source of the gods' power! It has to go back into place, so everything can be fixed."

Amy shakes her head. "I told you, Hannah. I said it from the start, I *hated* things the way they were. I want to go to St Mary's. The teachers there will treat me just like everyone else."

"But you were *helping* us!" I shout.

"I helped you stop Alastair because the objects are dangerous, that's all. I never wanted the marker stone to go back." She wipes her nose with her sleeve. "This is the only way I can be happy, Hannah! And you will be too, once you get used to it."

I shake my head so hard my hair slaps my cheeks. "I know my parents ignore me sometimes, but that doesn't mean I want them to be different *people*. I love them. You can't take my parents away from me and replace them with . . . boring humans."

Misery slides across Amy's face and the magpie on her shoulder puts its beak to her ear, almost as if it's talking to her. "I'm sorry, Hannah," she says, after a moment. "Soon you'll be human too and you won't remember anything different. *Then* you'll be happy."

"I *won't!*" I shout, as Amy turns back to Hermes, once more holding out the apple. Roses start growing around her feet.

"Again, Hermes!"

Hermes blasts the marker stone, making it jump and smash back into the pavement. How many more hits can it take before it shatters?

Then, above the hiss of the rain, I hear a clap of sound. Amy gapes at the green behind me and I turn.

Dolio is back . . . and he isn't alone. Dylan is holding one side of his shell. Alastair the other. They both look as if they have been dragged through a hurricane. Has Dolio *carried* them here? I had no idea he could do that.

Dylan lets go of Dolio, and staggers to one side. Alastair goes the other way.

"B-b-b-" he says, then he falls down.

"Dolio?" I gasp. "Dylan?" There is no sign of Elsie. "*Alastair!*"

Dylan drops on to the grass and looks up at the sky. "Woah."

"Dylan, *get up!*"

"I just flew," he says. "Dolio can *fly!*" He rolls and looks at me, and then at Amy. "What's going on?"

"Amy's trying to destroy the marker stone – she wants to stay human!"

"Oh!" Dylan clambers dizzily to his feet. Beside him Alastair is retching into the grass. "Amy, you can't do that." He reaches out a hand. "What about Elsie and Myrtle?"

Amy blinks away tears, and Myrtle coos loudly from her perch on the cross in the centre of the green.

"And what about your new power?" I shout. "Don't you want to know what else you can do with a whopping great sword? I bet you can *make* people treat you differently."

A laugh bursts out of Amy's chest as if she tried to suppress it. She whirls around. Alastair has tried to creep up on her other side.

"Watch out, Amy!" Dylan yells.

I turn to Dylan. "Alastair won't hurt her – Amy was on his side all along!"

"What?" Amy shakes her head. "No, I wasn't. Hermes, help!"

Hermes drops the thunderbolt and grabs Alastair, lifting him off his feet by his shoulders.

Dolio nudges my shoe and I bend down to pick him up. Rain streams from his shell and he looks meaningfully at the bag. "I don't know why you brought *Alastair*," I whisper, and I put him back inside.

Alastair wriggles in Hermes' hold, but Hermes is a god, so he has no chance of escape. Alastair twists in his grip, meeting my eyes. "Hannah, Amy won't listen to you until you get rid of the magpie!"

Dylan narrows his eyes. "Why should we believe *you*?"

"He doesn't want the marker destroyed," I say, thin-lipped. "Do you, Alastair? You still think you can use it to take the source of the gods' power."

Alastair sags in Hermes' grip. "I get why you'd think that, but ..." he groans. "When Dolio turned up and I realised you needed help, Hannah, I just . . . I grabbed his shell without even thinking. I-I know what I did was wrong . . ."

"You *think*?" Dylan shouts. "You nearly killed us!"

"The fire was an accident." Alastair sounds choked. "I meant there to be a lot of smoke to create a distraction, but it got out of control! I didn't know what to do."

I clench my fists. "What about hitting Hermes with the spear? You had no idea Dylan would be able to cure him. *And* you chained me to a rock."

"I know!" Alastair looks at Hermes. "I'm sorry!" Then he looks back at me. "I'm sorry for all of it. I just . . . wanted to be liked . . . loved, like my nan loved me. But while I was hiding from you guys, I realised that I wasn't as upset about the plan failing as I was about the fact I'd lost any chance I had of being friends with you."

He jerks his chin towards Amy. "You have to get that magpie away from her." Then he starts to cry. "It's making her focus on her misery. It's evil."

"Evil?" I look harder at the bird, which hunches into Amy's hair and returns my glare.

"It's not a magpie," Alastair says. "It's an emissary for the oldest of the gods."

Dylan moves to stand beside me. "What?"

Alastair swallows. "It happened after Nan died." He hangs his head. "Mum started worshipping her and . . . so did I." He touches his locket. "The whole thing was *her* idea. Taking the stone, taking the objects, finding the power source, giving it to the humans. I thought she was trying to help me, but now I think *I* was helping *her*."

Dylan stares. "It was your *mum's* idea?"

"No!" Alastair shakes his head. "You don't understand. Mum and I – we opened the door and *she* came through. The magpie's her physical form in this world."

"Whose physical form? You aren't making any sense!" I shout.

The magpie fluffs its wings and Alastair lowers his voice, so that I have to strain to hear him over the rain. The streetlight above him hisses and goes out, leaving Alastair and Hermes standing in near darkness.

"You saw her picture in Tartarus. It's the primordial," Alastair says, his voice emerging from the dark. "The Goddess of Darkness and Misery. Her name is Achlys."

CHAPTER THIRTY-TWO

"**A**CHLYS?"

Before I've finished saying the name, the ground trembles and I lose my balance. I fall to my knees, splashing into the mud. A cloud shifts and the moon comes out, revealing Amy backing towards the centre of the green. Myrtle is perched on the cross with her wings half-spread and an expression that would make me terrified to be airborne.

Amy takes one more step, holding the apple in front of her, and Myrtle launches herself from the cross, wings whistling, claws extended. She hurls herself at the magpie and Amy screams.

The magpie has dug its talons into Amy, but Myrtle hits it like a feathery torpedo and drags it off Amy's shoulder. The birds hit the ground in a whirlwind of feathers and Amy blinks.

"Myrtle!" She drops the arm holding the apple and its glow fades.

"Grandad!" I run towards the thunderbolt that lies on the

floor between us and he looks up, eyes no longer glazed, looking furious. Then the world . . . shifts.

Dylan shouts my name and I turn in time to see that, where there were two fighting birds, there is now a blackness that sucks the rain towards it, like gravity.

"*Ach-lys!*"

The word is so long and drawn out, I am not even sure it's a word. It's like a feeling, shivering in the air. I writhe with pain and clap my hands over my ears. Even through my shaking hands, I can hear what seems like the sobbing of a million souls; a wail of desolation that makes my stomach clench and sends a spike of pain through my heart.

Alastair curls up in a ball with his hands over his head.

Hermes races past me, heading towards the black hole, his wings beating so hard the rain is whipped into little hurricanes behind him. "Stay there, Hannah!" he yells. "*I'll* deal with this. You too, Dylan!" He shoves him towards me.

My best friend crashes into me and we both fall into the mud. Gasping, I wipe rain and tears from my eyes just in time to see Amy coming in fast. Hermes has thrown her after us. She lands on Dylan and Aphrodite's apple rolls from her hand.

Dolio crawls out of my bag and goes after Hermes.

I scramble free of my friends, to see Hermes taking hold of Dolio. He says something I can't hear and tosses him back to us. I catch him in my midriff.

"Stay out of the way, kids," Hermes calls, with no trace of mischief in his expression. "Only a god can stop her."

Dolio bites my finger so hard I drop him. He hurtles back towards Hermes, but he is too late.

Hermes tears his staff from his belt, lifts it over his head and flings himself into the black hole.

The hole closes over him and vanishes.

Dolio stops still, a domed shape huddled on the green.

Silence gathers around us.

For a moment, the world seems to hold its breath. Then the rain begins to lighten, until it is nothing more than a drizzle. The clouds shift, revealing a full moon that bathes us in light.

"That storm was brought by . . . Achlys?" Dylan says.

All that is left where Hermes vanished is his lonely old tortoise and a huddled pile of pale feathers.

Ignoring the mud that smears her from top to toe, Amy crawls towards it. "Myrtle?" She picks up her dove and cradles her in her palms. She looks at me with horrified eyes. "I think she's—"

The black hole reopens behind her. On her knees, Amy turns, still holding Myrtle. I raise the thunderbolt but, coming from behind, Alastair tackles me into the mud.

To my shock, when I struggle, Dylan lands adds his weight to Alastair's. "*Hermes* couldn't stop her," he yells. "What do you think *you* can do?"

Amy stares, frozen, and I can do nothing but watch as Dolio crawls in front of her, as if he can protect her, and the sound of misery once more fills the air.

Then the hole condenses, the blackness inside it deepening. It changes shape and darkens until, instead of a hole, there is a cloaked figure standing beside Amy. The moonlight highlights the hunch of her shoulders, her swollen knees, nails long as claws. Her nose is dripping and blood stains her cheeks. She sees us staring and grins.

Then she peers at Alastair, with the blood dribbling down her face. "Hello, my boy," she whispers, and her voice is the trembling of civilisations. "You failed me!" Her grin fades. "I gave you a foolproof plan, donated my strength to enable you to move the stone, and still you failed me." Her long nails come up to point and Alastair whimpers. "With your help, the humans were going to destroy *themselves*," she says. "Now, it's up to me."

"I *knew* he didn't move the marker on his own!" I whisper to Dylan. Then I raise my voice. "What have you done to Hermes?"

Achlys turns her gaze on me, and I immediately regret seeking her attention. She meets my eyes and I find myself falling into a well of sadness.

My parents never paid much attention to me, even before Henry was born. Dylan is only my friend because everyone else thinks he's weird. Amy hates me. My powers are pointless. In a village filled with gods and their families, I am nothing special, nothing notable, nothing interesting . . . Nothing.

Alastair slaps a hand over my eyes and breaks the connection. "Don't let her into your head!" he hisses. "You aren't nothing – you are Hannah hecking Messenger! If anyone can get us out of this, it's you!"

Ignoring the sobbing Amy, Achlys glides forward. "Time can be funny, can't it? Days can seem short or long, minutes can turn into hours, hours into moments. When you are miserable, time drags and drags, doesn't it, Alastair?" Her voice is the whistle of a kettle, and the darkness settles around her like a cloak.

Alastair nods.

"I've returned Hermes to the place he was most miserable. Tartarus. For him, it's already been centuries. Centuries chained once more to that rock."

"No!" I gasp.

She tilts her head and blood drips from her cheeks. "Still, he hasn't broken. Of course, he doesn't have to. *Rock*. That's what my magpie heard him say. *You* thought it meant a diamond, Alastair!" She laughs. "Now, I know where the power source is."

"Alastair, this is all your fault!" I kick him and he rolls off me.

Achlys turns back to me, and I cover my eyes again. "You should be grateful, little worm." I hear her coming closer. "You think *you're* unhappy? You should hear the humans. Eight *billion* souls screaming into the dark. Rich and poor. Young and old. Endlessly miserable, and I've been able to do nothing for them. Me – the *Goddess* of Misery."

She walks past, and I drop my hand to watch her approach the marker stone, the source of the gods' power.

"Your gods stole my worshippers," she says. "Did you know that every time a primordial's name is spoken, it strengthens them?" She looks at me, but I don't meet her eye.

I shake my head. Dylan squeezes my hand.

"And did you know that the longer a primordial goes without hearing their name, the weaker they grow?"

"We didn't know," Dylan calls.

Achlys ignores him. "I was made into nothing but a whisper on the wind." She touches her own cheek as if she can barely believe it is real. "But every single human tear hurts me. Can you imagine how that feels?"

She exhales and, for a moment, I can imagine just how awful that would be. I wrap my arms around my chest. "I-I'm sorry."

"I managed to regain just enough strength, through the pain, to whisper to Alastair's mother, deep in her grief. To give her my name. Since then, day-by-day, I've been growing stronger and now, thanks to Alastair, I am back."

He hangs his head.

"Once I am finished," Achlys says, "there will be no more pain, and no more tears, because there will be no one left to cry!" She touches the stone. "Finally!" Her grin is awful. "Don't be sad, children, it'll be over quickly." She gestures to the sky. "I think I will blot out the sun, moon and stars. There will be a great darkness. An eternal darkness."

The moonlight dims and I look up. Half of the moon has vanished, as if a chunk has been bitten out of it. It is the same shape as Achlys' grin.

CHAPTER THIRTY-TWO

AMY MOVES first. She lies Myrtle beneath the cross, wrapping her wings around her little body. Dolio crawls to the dove and huddles beside her, head pulled into his shell, as if he's mourning. Then Amy thrusts her hand into the air and grabs Aphrodite's sword.

"You promised me I could be *normal*," she shouts. "You lied!"

She clambers to her feet and stalks forwards, swinging the sword.

"Amy, *no!*" Dylan starts, but I hold him back.

"Let Amy distract Achlys! I'll protect the stone. Can you get help?"

"How?" Dylan looks terrified.

"You speak to the dead," I shout. "*You* work it out!"

Achlys turns her grin on Amy and I run to the left, out of her line of sight. I look back once to see Alastair whispering urgently in Dylan's ear.

I don't know how much time Amy can buy me, or if she can keep Achlys' attention any longer than Hermes did, so I have to move as fast as I can. I leave Dylan and Alastair to their plotting, hoping that they can come up with something good.

I push Zeus's thunderbolt into my belt loop and banish the stupid human thoughts, which are still – even in the face of a primordial attempting to destroy the world – telling me I'm a normal girl. I try to find a sense of calm. If I ever needed control of my power, it's now.

I inhale, exhale, inhale, exhale, and my power responds, lifting me from the ground.

I stretch my arms like I did in the shed, to help me fly as fast as I possibly can. Air rushes by me, chilling my nose and cheeks, and my hair whips behind me in wet ropes. I circle behind Achlys and the stone.

You can't see me, I think. *There's nobody here.*

The gloom is deepening, and I shiver as I land a few steps from the marker and edge closer as quickly and stealthily as I can. Amy has reached Achlys and she strikes at her with the sword, but Achlys simply waves a hand and a barrier appears between them. Sparks fly wherever Amy's weapon lands. Achlys keeps her gaze on Amy as she laughs.

I drop to a crouch; the stone is just out of my reach. I stretch out my fingers. Achlys starts to turn.

"Achlys!" Dylan's voice rings out. "I have someone who wants to talk to you!"

I stare as he puts out a hand and turns his fist as if he is opening a door. An old woman steps through, her outline surrounded by a fuzzy radiance. Dylan makes another gesture and closes the invisible door, leaving her standing at his side.

The old lady looks at Dylan, then at Alastair, then at Achlys. "Oh yes," she says. "I have a few things to say, all right!"

"Nan!" Alastair launches himself at the shining figure. He flies straight through her and stumbles to a halt. Then he turns back around. "Nan?"

"I can hear you, dear." The old woman frowns. "I can't hold you, I'm sorry. You have your mum for that."

"Not since you . . . went," Alastair cries. "It's been—"

"I know." The old lady looks sad. "You've made some bad choices. But you aren't a bad person." She looks at Achlys. "*You*, however . . ."

Once again, Achlys turns her back on me and I release a breath. I put my hand on the stone.

It's only a stone, cold and wet, rough against my skin. I slide my palm across the surface until I feel the indents of the ram's head carving. My fingertips are barely a centimetre from Achlys' ridged nails.

Then I close my eyes and try to remember the sensation of falling into it.

Nothing happens. Probably because I'm still awake and conscious.

"I come from Zeus," I whisper.

I feel a tingle, but I'm not flooded with the power of the gods. It's not working!

How did Dylan manage to access the power when he fixed Hermes?

Of course, he was holding the spear.

My eyes flick to the thunderbolt in my belt. With one hand on the stone, I close the other around the lightning.

"I come from Zeus," I say again.

This time power slams into me. My head is thrown back and I bite back a scream.

This is the power of the gods.

Channelling the thunderbolt, I sling a wave of energy towards Achlys, flinging her from the stone and away from Amy, who is still wielding her sword. Then, while Achlys is still trying to regain her footing, facing away from me, I create a dozen other marker stones and send them spinning around her. I hecking *love* being a trickster, after all!

The real stone, I disguise as a bush. It's the first thing that comes to mind.

"Which of these is real?" Achlys shrieks, lunging at one and then another. "Tell me, or I will visit such misery upon you!"

Amy stumbles towards Dylan and I use all the power at my command to lift the marker stone. The stone/bush wobbles a few centimetres above the ground, like a sagging balloon, until I realise it would be better if Achlys could not see it at all. I turn us both invisible and push it carefully along the edge of the field, trying to block out the sound of Achlys, who screams each time she puts hands on a fake.

Finally, I reach the boundary. Despite the mud and the

darkness, I can still see the bare spot where the stone has rested for decades. I manoeuvre it into place and let it drop.

Then I remove my hand.

It happens in a blink. I close my eyes, and when I reopen them, Hockwold is no longer human. The real Hockwold Hall is etched against the stars, pillars and all. The church steeple has vanished and been replaced by the temple to Zeus.

My mind no longer feels balanced on a knife edge. My human memories vanish like fog in the sun, and I feel comfortable in my own brain for the first time in hours.

The marker stone is once more working in sync with the boundary spell, rather than inside it.

Dylan whoops and I turn around. He's giving me a thumbs up.

It felt like a victory, getting the marker stone back in place. But, when Achlys whips around and heads towards me, quick as a blur, I realise that what I've done is show her which marker stone was real. It will hardly matter that I've returned Hockwold to normal, if Achlys gets hold of the power source and destroys the sun.

Her grin expands as she draws nearer.

Amy, Dylan and Alastair run after her, but Achlys is faster. She swipes her filthy nails at my face, and I duck and lose my grip on the stone. I stagger backwards.

You can't see me, I think. *I'm not here.* It's almost impossible to remain calm, but I try to find some zen. Come on, powers, don't fail me now.

Achlys turns, straining to seek me out, like a vulture.

She can't see me.

She sniffs the air. I tiptoe backwards.

Then Achlys shrugs and lays her hands on the stone. She mutters something, and I look up to see the moon vanishing, bite by bite.

"Oh, Hera," I whisper. "What do we do? And where's Zeus? Shouldn't he be here by now?"

Alastair's nan appears at my side; she's hardly more than an impression in the air now, as if Dylan is too weak to hold her here.

She leans closer and her voice tickles my ear. "I have a message for you," she breathes. "Destroy the locket! It was mine, so Alastair won't let it go, but it represents his grief. That's what is holding Achlys in this world. He has to let go of it."

Then she vanishes, like a party candle blown out.

The moon is nothing more than a sliver now and the clouds have returned, the rain getting harder, as if the sky itself is crying.

I run to meet Alastair, Dylan and Amy as Achlys laughs at us.

"Sorry, Alastair."

I rip the locket from his throat. He yells in surprise and tries to get it back. I jump out of reach, then I fit my thumbnail into the side and flip it open. A black and white magpie's feather flutters out and is snatched by the breeze. Amy catches it between her finger and thumb.

"Alastair?" I say. "You have to do this."

He starts to cry, sobs that make his chest heave. But he pulls a book of matches out of his trouser pocket. As Achlys eats the last part of the moon, replacing it with her endless darkness, Alastair takes a match and scrapes it against the sandpaper, igniting the tiny flame.

It flares and he holds it to one edge of the feather.

It catches light, the vanes blackening, the fluff curling and turning to ash.

Achlys screams, lifts her claws from the stone and flies towards us.

I drop the locket on the grass. Then I grasp Zeus's thunderbolt and slam it down right in the centre of the silver frame. There is a bang and a bright light. I close my eyes.

When I open them again, there is no sign of Achlys.

There is only a magpie feather lying on the grass between us.

CHAPTER THIRTY-THREE

AMY IS the first to speak.

"It's so dark." She wraps her arms around herself. "Has she gone?"

"I think so," I say. But the damage Achlys did remains: the moon is all but gone.

Alastair is still crying.

I bend over, pick up the remains of the locket and hand it to him. "Sorry, Alastair," I say. "I know that was your nan's."

He nods.

Dylan puts a hand on his shoulder. "If you like . . . I can let you talk to her every now and again. You know, when you need to."

Alastair's eyes widen. "You'd do that?" He shuffles his feet. "I-I thought you'd never want to speak to me again. Aren't you going to hand me over to Zeus?"

Amy shakes her head. "We *should*." Her shoulders slump. "But

I've had Achlys in my head too now. I know how persuasive she is. And anyway, Hermes said he'd take the blame."

"Grandad!" I cry. "He's back in Tartarus. We have to get him out!"

Dylan catches my arm. "We will, but . . . what about the world? The moon?" He points upwards. "What does it mean?"

I look up with a shiver. "Endless darkness, that's what she said."

Dylan claps a hand over my mouth. "Don't say her name!"

I nod.

"Hannah," Amy says. "Is there *anything* you can do – with the marker stone, maybe?"

"I don't know." There's a tiny thunderclap and Dolio is perched on the stone, looking meaningfully at me. "I guess Dolio thinks there's something."

We head across the green and stand around the stone.

"I do know I can't do this alone," I say, holding out a hand in front of me.

Amy doesn't move. "I tried to destroy the stone," she said. "I wanted to stay human."

"I know," I say.

Dylan takes her hand. "I don't really get it, you wanting to be treated like everyone else. But, if the world doesn't end and we have to go back to school, we can start a campaign to make the teachers treat you more fairly. I'll throw a strop about how you always get a good mark even when your work is rubbish."

Amy smiles tremulously. "You'd do that?"

I nod. "We can make posters, if you like."

Dylan grins. "*A Fair Grade for Fairchild!* What do you think?"

Amy sniffs.

"Hannah can throw a monstrous wobbly," Dylan says.

"Yup," I say. "I'll throw stuff."

Amy laughs and Dylan places her hand on top of mine above the stone. We stand there, the three of us, hands piled together.

Only Alastair stands apart.

I turn to him. "I know we aren't your nan. But we can be your friends."

Alastair wipes his nose on his sleeve. "You *really* don't hate me?"

I shake my head. "We all treated you badly. Ignored you. It's as much our fault as yours. And you were under the influence of a primordial goddess! Do you forgive us?"

"Of course." His eyes are wide with surprise.

"Then bring in your hand," Amy says.

Alastair hesitates, and then places his hand on top of Dylan's.

I take a deep breath, and then I put my free hand on the thunderbolt and nod. We drop our joined hands on to the stone.

"We come from Zeus," I say.

Energy runs through me like a bolt of electricity, and I open my eyes to find myself back inside the marker. This time the mist surrounding me is murky and bleak and filled with the feeling of sadness. The glimmering specks that once hung in the air have sunk and now cling to my feet. But I am not alone. I can feel Dylan, Amy and Alastair, their hands on mine, their own energy each unique.

Dylan has a purple aura, and around him is a sense of happiness.

The excitement of a birthday party, the thrill of a graduation, the joy of a wedding. But beneath the celebration that surrounds him is something deeper: the somberness of a funeral, and the voices of the dead wanting to be heard. His power is about limits and what happens when you remove them.

Amy is pastel pink. Around her is love: love of family and love of friends. But beneath that is something darker: love of self, love of things, covetousness and jealousy. Love in all its forms might be the most dangerous power of all. I see why she gets a sword.

I look at Alastair, expecting to see nothing. A human. But Alastair wears an orange glow. Around him is heat: the roaring flame.

No wonder he couldn't control the blaze he set in the tree. Alastair Ignatius, descendant of Prometheus, has a connection to fire. But it isn't just destruction. He contains the warmth of a hearth and the sharing of good food.

Warmth, love, happiness. What do I bring? I look down at myself. My aura is grey. I sigh. Of course it is.

I hear Amy. "Look closer, Hannah."

So, I do. My aura *is* grey, but it isn't drab. Grey is made up of all the other colours; they swirl through me, lighting me like a rainbow. My power is about communication, connection and bringing people together. Sometimes it's by taking messages, sometimes it's by playing tricks.

Warmth, love, happiness, connection.

That's what the four of us create when we're united. That's what we can bring to the world. Not darkness, but light.

I focus, allowing my aura to radiate outwards, encompassing first Dylan's, then Amy's, then Alastair's. We shine inside the source of the gods' power, lightening Achlys' gloom.

For a moment nothing happens, then the glimmering specks around our feet rise and surround us like stars. The mist lightens and the feeling of despair vanishes.

"Not eternal darkness," I say. "Not death, not misery. But light and life and connection." Then I open my eyes.

The sun is rising.

Dolio appears to be smirking, in so far as a tortoise can smirk.

Dylan drops his hands from ours. "Hannah, what time is it? Wasn't it nighttime a minute ago?"

Amy retrieves her own hand and swipes her hair out of her face. "That can't have taken hours, can it?"

I look at my watch and frown. "It should be almost midnight."

"Yes – it should." The voice of Zeus crackles through the air and I squeak embarrassingly, jumping away from the marker stone like it's burnt me.

Zeus stands in front of his huge metal gate, hands on his hips, iron-grey hair whipping in the dawn breeze. His jaw is set, his lips narrowed and his eyes are swirling with silver specks like stars.

Dylan gulps and Amy slips behind him.

Zeus looks at me. "Hannah Messenger, isn't that *my* thunderbolt?"

CHAPTER THIRTY-FOUR

ZEUS HAS barely finished speaking before the other residents of Hockwold start to appear. And they do *not* look happy.

Mum is at the front of the crowd, holding Henry. The moment she spots me, she starts yelling.

"Hannah, what have you been *doing*? What happened to our memories? Why has your father been counting cars? What happened to the *world*?" She shudders. "I've been sending emails, Hannah! *Emails*. I feel dirty. What in Hera's name is going on?"

Mr Prince emerges from Hockwold Hall, along with Zack and Zane. Zack looks like he's been sick. He points at Dylan. "I told you he'd be involved," he shouts.

Other phrases emerge from the general hum of alarm.

"Knew they were trouble . . ."

"Related to Hermes, of course . . ."

"That awful boy . . ."

"Surprised to see Amy Fairchild with them . . ."

"Hang on a minute, that's my daughter you're talking about!" Dad pushes from behind Amy's confused-looking mum and stands in front of us. His mouth flattens and, for the first time, I see the resemblance to Hermes.

His wings emerge from his ankle socks and flutter, boosting him up a few centimetres and giving him some height.

"Wow, your dad's *really* mad," Dylan whispers.

I nod. "But not at us."

Dad turns and looks at me, as if he's seeing me for the first time. "Whatever it is," he says, "I'm on your side." And he folds his arms.

"Wow, Dad. Thanks."

My hair stands on end. I rub my arms and static forms along my fingers. Silence falls over the green as Zeus strides forward.

"Dawn at midnight, Hannah?" He tilts his head. "The world feels a little . . . off."

I swallow. "It would be. It was . . ." I lower my voice. "Actually, I can't say her name . . . it's a bad idea . . . um . . ."

I pick up Dolio and hug him tightly, trying not to squash him against the thunderbolt.

Alastair takes a deep breath and steps forward. "It was me, it was my fault."

"Shut up, Alastair," Amy snaps. "No, it wasn't." She lifts her sword and stands in front of him. "We fought the Eternal Darkness, we can fight *you*!"

Zeus's eyes widen. "Ah, good morning little Fairchild."

Amy's mum collapses into someone's arms.

"Amy's right," I say. "It wasn't Alastair's fault, or any of ours. It was *yours*."

Dylan and Amy look horrified. "What are you *saying*, Hannah?" Dylan hisses.

"The Goddess of Misery told us you left her powerless," I say. I straighten and hold the thunderbolt at my side. "You replaced her and then you let humanity just get more and more unhappy. Now there are eight *billion* miserable humans calling out in pain and she came back because of it and almost destroyed the world just to shut them up. This is *your* fault."

Zeus's hand closes over mine and, as Dad squares his shoulders, he unfurls my fingers from the thunderbolt.

"It's all right, Herman," he says. Then he kneels in front of me. "Hannah Messenger, I know the goddess you are talking about. Eternal darkness, Goddess of Misery, the primordial." He pauses. "You're right, we won't say her name. And we couldn't just take over and do what she used to. Those who earnt her attention were gifted the ability to take vengeance on those who had wronged them." He leans closer. "Now, can you imagine eight billion people taking revenge on each other?"

"I . . ." I fall silent, and hug Dolio closer.

"That's right." He smiles. "There's a reason her son was named Chaos."

"But . . . look what happened," Amy says. "Why didn't you do something for the humans?"

"We did." Zeus stands and gestures towards the crowd. "We gave them stories. Stories about gods, demi-gods, heroes defeating monsters. We gave them stories to tell around the fireside, teaching them lessons, making them happy, giving them hope." He spreads his hands. "We have given the humans stories for centuries. We have held the darkness at bay for hundreds of years." He looks sad. "Of course, humans are so *determined* to make one another unhappy."

"And the stories aren't working any more?" Dylan says.

Zeus shrugs. "It's up to a new generation to come up with ways to inspire and create hope." He looks at me. "Dawn at midnight might be a good start."

"W-w-what?" The human from before, stands up from behind the temple wall. The temple that had been St Peter's church a few minutes earlier. "I was taking rubbings inside the church, out of the rain . . . and then it wasn't a church any more and you . . . and you . . ." he points, his eyes are round, his cheeks bloodless. "I saw . . ."

"Well," Dylan's mum says, widening her eyes meaningfully at Zeus. "I'm not surprised you're seeing things, if you've been out all night in this storm. Come with me, dear. I'm sure they can do you some breakfast at the Red Lion. A nice cup of tea will help you make sense of everything."

We all remain silent as Mrs Vine takes the man's arm and leads him out past the marker stone and into Wilton. The moment he passes the stone, his shoulders relax and he looks back, the tension leaving his face. "You know," he says, as Mrs Vine propels him towards the pub, "I must have fallen asleep on one of the pews. I had the strangest dream."

Zeus nods with satisfaction, takes his thunderbolt and turns to go back towards his gate.

"Wait!" Amy calls. She drops her sword and picks up her dove. Myrtle lies in Amy's palm, her head flopping, her wings limp. "Is there *anything* you can do? Please?"

Zeus stays still for a moment, then he takes Myrtle from Amy's hand. "A brave soul, indeed, and filled with love." He sighs and then he presses a kiss to Myrtle's breast.

Myrtle coos weakly, then she lifts her head. Zeus releases her and she flutters towards Amy's shoulder. She settles, nibbles Amy's ear and poops down her back. Amy laughs.

Dylan raises his own hand. "What about Hermes?"

"Hermes?" Zeus frowns. "*Hermes* has something to do with this?"

"He tried to stop Ach . . . I mean, the eternal darkness," Dylan says. "She sent him away."

"I think he's back in Tartarus." I look at Dad and wince.

"*Back* in Tartarus?" Dad snaps. "When was he *not* in Tartarus?"

"He tried to save us," I say, and face Zeus. "You should let him out."

Zeus puts a hand on his hip. "Should I?"

Amy looks belligerent. "*She* made him believe he's been down there for centuries. So he's been punished plenty, hasn't he?"

Zeus peers from Amy's determined face to Dolio, who is wrapped in my arms.

Then he raises his thunderbolt and slashes it downwards. A rip appears in the air, revealing a rock, where Hermes is once more chained.

"Hermes!" Amy shouts.

Hermes raises his head and spots Zeus. He looks exhausted; his eyes sunken, his chest still blackened, his shirt in tatters. "Hello, Father," he says.

Zeus gestures and his chains vanish. "Come on then," he says. "Out of there. But no more tricks."

Hermes stumbles to his feet and glares at the rock behind him. "OK. But first, can I borrow your thunderbolt? This is one rock I *can* blow up."

CHAPTER
THIRTY-FIVE

WE ARE all in my bedroom. It's back to normal; a tatty, Pegasus-themed room with a scorched rug.

Dylan lies on the pull-out bed with Elsie and Alastair, and Amy and I sit cross-legged on mine. She has Myrtle and I am holding Dolio.

"I'm going to need a pet too," Alastair says, thoughtfully.

"How about you guys share Elsie," I say. "She has got two heads after all."

Alastair laughs, just as the whole house rocks. Cracks appear in the wall behind Dylan, and Dolio moves under the duvet so fast that my hand drops on to the bed with a thump. A sound like thunder rolls through the room and I lurch to my feet. "Mum? Dad?"

Amy leaps up after me and Dylan follows with Elsie. There's a crunch, and the ceiling shivers. Dylan grabs my arm.

"Didn't your mum put Henry down for a nap?"

As he says it, my brother starts to scream.

"*Henry!*"

We sprint from my room, almost tripping on the floor, as the boards undulate under the carpet. Amy grabs Dylan for support and my magic coughs, lifting me into midair. I take a calming breath, then I fly for the nursery and fling open the door.

Henry is standing in his cot, howling. He is gripping the bars, his hair a mass of messy black curls, his cheeks flushed.

Above him, the ceiling is cracked and the light is swaying dangerously. Mum appears at the top of the stairs. "*Henry!*"

There's a creak, and the light starts to break away from its plaster fitting, right over Henry's head.

I've never moved so fast in my life. My wings beat and I fly from the doorway to the cot and back before my heart can thud once in my chest. I have Henry in my arms, his legs dangling. He clings to my hair and stares at me, his howling silenced, his eyes wide. Then the pendant tears from the ceiling and slams into his mattress in an explosion of dust and blankets.

"Henry!" Mum stumbles down the hall, which is still moving. Dylan and Amy reach my side and Dylan pulls my feet to the ground. It feels as if I'm standing on a ship, the whole place rocking. Alastair is holding on to Elsie in the doorway.

"What's happening?" Amy shouts. "Is it … *her* … again?"

Mum shakes her head. "I think it's Herman."

"Dad?" I gape at her and then look up. The cracks in the ceiling are emanating from a central spot, like a cobweb. They are coming from the spare room.

"Herman!" Mum shouts and, leaving Henry with me, she turns and runs.

"Get the fire extinguisher!" I yell to the others, as I go after her.

"Where is it?" Amy calls.

"Kitchen," Dylan says. "Come on."

The other three reel towards the stairs as Mum pulls open the spare room door. I am right behind her, just in time to see Dad floating in the centre of a whirlwind of ashes.

"Dad!"

"Herman, what have you done?" Mum shouts.

The whirlwind pulls away from Dad and he is dumped on the floor, landing on hands and knees and staring upwards. The dust keeps swirling, the movement getting tighter and denser, until it looks almost solid.

There's a rustling, and then Dolio is sitting on the dressing table. One thing has survived the chaos: a bunch of fake flowers that Mum keeps in a vase. Dolio is chewing on them, and he looks utterly disgusted.

A pounding on the stairs announces Dylan and Amy. "We've got it!" Amy shouts, brandishing the fire extinguisher.

"I don't think we need it this time," Mum says. She points.

The dust is forming a shape. A human shape.

"Is that . . . Hera?" Amy whispers.

"I . . . think so." I settle Henry on to my hip. He is watching the dust with fascination as he chews on a handful of my hair. "I think Dolio would be more worried if it wasn't."

As one, we turn to watch Dolio, who is now pushing the vase

of fake flowers towards the edge of the dresser with single-minded determination.

Mum reaches out too late to grab the vase. It teeters on the edge and falls, to smash on the floor, just as the dust settles.

"I did it!" Dad yells.

And the woman who is standing, naked, in the middle of the destruction, smiles at him.

Amy claps her hand over Dylan's eyes and Mum whips off her long cardigan. She passes it to Hera, who takes it and puts it on, closing it and tying the belt.

Amy takes her hand away from Dylan's face.

Hera is beautiful. Not *Aphrodite* beautiful, obviously, but she looks exactly like you thought your mum, or your other favourite grown-up, looked when you were little. When you *knew* they were the most wonderful person in the whole universe, and you couldn't imagine anyone being more perfect. Her hair is in a long plait that winds around her head, and her eyes are full of kindness.

Mum falls to her knees and we quickly follow.

"Hera," she says, pressing her forehead against the ground.

I glance up. Hera is smiling.

"Do get up," she says. She looks around the room. "It's a bit of mess in here, isn't it?"

Mum flushes and Hera holds out a hand. Dolio blurs and then appears on her palm, looking up at her with Testudine adoration. Hera brushes a hand over his shell and suddenly, for the first time I can remember, he's clean. The dust that he has been wearing for years is gone. Hera wipes her hand on her cheek and the dust stays there for a moment, a shadowy line, then it is absorbed into her skin.

She gives him a kiss and hands him to me. "Thank you, Dolio," she says. She looks at the dove on Amy's shoulder. "And thank you too, Myrtle," she says. "And, of course, the brave Elsie." She pats her on the heads.

I stare at Hera. "What . . .?"

"Dolio has very kindly been helping me keep an eye on things," Hera says. "And it's a good job too."

She frowns and turns to Dad. "Herman, I said I wanted a rest. I don't appreciate your trying to wake me up every five minutes."

Dad flushes. "We needed you, Hera. The minute you left, the council started meeting. They've been discussing getting involved in human politics, which would be a disaster!"

Hera frowns. "What does Zeus say?"

"Nothing since you left," Mum snaps. Then she hangs her head. "Sorry, Hera."

"All right, I'll deal with him." She turns to me. "You've been having quite the adventure, haven't you, granddaughter of Hermes?"

Suddenly Mum frowns. "Where *is* Hermes?"

Hera closes her eyes, her smile widens, then she opens them again. "My stepson is in the kitchen, watching a screen, with headphones on his ears." She laughs gently. "He hasn't even noticed I'm back." Then she purses her lips. "But he will." She turns back to me. "So, Hannah Messenger, you have touched the power of the gods and learnt that you can be more than they tell you.

That our power is more than just …" she glances at Dylan's pocket, "party tricks and sweets."

Dylan flushes and shuffles his feet.

"You have done incredibly well. It seems that my great-grandchildren are more than powerful enough to deal with any future problems that may arise." She looks at me again.

No, she isn't looking at me. She's looking at Henry. He grins at her and holds up a handful of my hair as if to offer her some of the delicious snack.

"No thank you, Henry darling," she says. She stretches. "I suppose I'd better go and see my husband and put a stop to all the silliness." She starts towards the door. Then she stops beside me. She hesitates, then places a kiss on my cheek.

"Hannah Messenger, you are a real hero."

CHAPTER
THIRTY-SIX

THE FOUR of us are walking to school: Amy, Dylan, Alastair and me. Five, if you count Dolio. Six, if you count Elsie. Seven, if you count Myrtle. Which I don't. I narrow my eyes at her, and she glowers back.

I am wearing a belt around my jeans. It has a paracord attachment. If my Zen fails and my power goes wild, the plan is I release the cord and one of the others catches it. We've been practising. It makes me feel like a human balloon, but Dad says it's ingenious and that he spent half his teenage years wearing lead boots.

Hermes is still at home. He saw us off at the door this morning, then went back to his television. He's finished watching *Teen Titans* and is now on *Stranger Things*. He says the upside-down reminds him of Tartarus and he's a little homesick. I'm getting worried, to be honest. I mean, twenty years of TV is a lot to catch up on, but it won't keep him occupied for ever. I suspect that the thwarting of pranks will loom large in my future. I just hope I can stop Zeus and Hera finding out about them.

"Awright, saddos!" It's Zack.

He and Zane stroll up to us, but instead of laughing at his brother, Zane nudges Zack and whispers something in his ear. Zack stiffens. "Right." He fidgets awkwardly. "My dad says that without you we'd all be boring humans, so I've got to be nice." He curls a lip. Then he shrugs. "But that doesn't mean I have to spend *time* with you losers. Come on, Amy." He starts towards the end of the road, then pauses when he realises that Amy hasn't followed. Nor has Zane.

"Come *on*, Amy!"

"Actually, I like spending time with the losers," Amy calls.

Zane remains, looking between Amy and his brother. He flushes.

I nudge Dylan, who catches my eye, grins and reaches into his pocket. "Here." He hands him a handful of strawberry laces. "And there's a special one for Zack."

"Come *on*, Zane!" Zack yells.

Zane smiles awkwardly at Dylan and then runs after his brother. We watch as he gives him his strawberry lace, as they turn the corner. Dylan clenches a fist.

There's a horrified yell from the next street.

"Did you just turn that lace into a *snake*?" Amy asks.

Dylan smirks. "Just a slow worm."

Amy takes his hand.

I look at the two of them. Alastair nudges me and Dolio sticks his head out of the bag. I pat it. "Yeah, I know," I say. "But it was only one *little* trick."

ACKNOWLEDGEMENTS

I CAN'T TELL you how much I enjoyed writing *Hannah Messenger* for you. *Hannah Messenger* is my first novel for your age group – up until now I've been writing for older teens and adults. I got to a point when I needed some humour and magic in my life, and that was when Hannah popped into my head, along with her exploding great-grandmother.

At a time when everything seemed a little dark and gloomy, meeting Hannah enabled me to rediscover my love of writing. I hope she brings you some humour and magic too.

Of course, Hannah didn't appear from nowhere. One of the best things about being a mum is all the hilarious anecdotes you accumulate, and Maisie and Riley (my own two troublemakers) were inspirational. Oh, the stories I could tell you (I won't – they would murder me – but, needless to say, the bucket of gravel and the indoor trampoline was something that really happened!). So, a big thank you to my own kids for being kind, funny and completely wonderful (although I wasn't pleased about picking gravel out of the carpet at the time).

Thanks also, as always, to my husband Andy, my agent Catherine Pellegrino and, of course, to the amazing team at UCLan Publishing. Especially Hazel Holmes who believed in Hannah, and my awesome editor Tilda Johnson, who shaped the novel into something you'd want to read.

If you want to find out more about the Greek gods, then do run to your librarian; there are so many brilliant books about them, and the old stories are fabulous.

And if you want to read the whole of Dylan's poem, the one he uses to remember who all the gods are, then here it is:

Number one, at the top, is Zeus the king.
Hera's the goddess who wears his ring.
Poseidon, his brother, is God of the Sea,
From which came the beautiful Aphrodite.
Athena, most wise, emerged from his head.
Another brother, Hades, rules the world of the dead.
Dionysus is god for parties with bunting.
Artemis is best if you want to go hunting.
Her twin, bright Apollo, is God of the Sun,
But if you want a fight, Ares is the one.
Demeter's cool if you want to grow food.
Hermes the Messenger's tricksy and rude.
Now you know them all, it's easy to see,
There's nothing so twisted as Zeus's family tree!

Perhaps you can write your own poem about the Greek gods, or a story about the day you found your own power (I wonder what it might be?).

And don't forget to fill your lives with humour, magic and good friends.

Love from,

Bryony